Kuani
Gillenwater
Mr. Myers

7/6/89

DREAM BOY

ESPECIALLY FOR GIRLS™ presents

DREAM BOY

Original Title: The First Time

Ann Reit

DELL PUBLISHING COMPANY

Weekly Reader Books offers several exciting
card and activity programs. For information,
write to WEEKLY READER BOOKS, P.O. Box 16636
Columbus, Ohio 43216.

This book is a presentation of Especially for Girls™, Weekly Reader Books.
Weekly Reader Books offers book clubs for children from preschool through high
school. For further information write to: **Weekly Reader Books**,
4343 Equity Drive, Columbus, Ohio 43228

Especially for Girls™
is a trademark of Weekly Reader Books.

Edited for Weekly Reader Books
and published by arrangement with
Dell Publishing Co., Inc.

Published by
Dell Publishing Co., Inc.
1 Dag Hammarskjold Plaza
New York, New York 10017

ISBN: 0-440-92560-6
Printed in the United States of America

DREAM BOY

CHAPTER *1*

When Gwen Warren woke up that Saturday morning in the beginning of April, she knew that the seemingly endless, grueling winter was over. Somewhere, not too far off, summer was hovering. She felt it in the warm sun that was on her face. Although she hadn't opened her eyes yet, she was aware of a bright light covering her bed, making little lacy patterns on the green quilt. The breeze coming in the open window carried the salty, pungent smell of the sea, which was only ten miles away.

Gwen stretched her legs, her toes reaching the bottom of the sheets that had been untouched all night. She wiggled her feet and moved them over the white coolness. Then she opened her eyes and raised her arms as far over her head as she could, making soft groans as she did. She looked around her room, admiring the white walls and white-wicker furniture and the pink and red drapes and bedspread. She had done it all herself, buying old furniture and painting it white and finding on sale just the right remnants of fabric to make the drapes. She didn't always like the practical side of herself, but sometimes it paid off.

Stretching one more luxurious time, she swung her legs over the bed and sat on its edge. She looked at her reflection in a mirror on the closet door opposite and thought, *Not bad. Not sensational but not bad.* Her head of reddish-brown, thick curly hair caught the rays of the sun, and her deep-brown eyes objectively admired the long legs that extended from the extra-large man's T-shirt she wore at night.

In the bathroom, she cupped her hands and threw icy cold water on her face, shivering and yelling. Then she ran down the stairs barefooted, silently, and stood in the doorway to the kitchen. She looked at her mother who sat at a table, a cigarette dangling from her lips, going through a cookbook. For a timeless, objective moment she saw her mother as a separate person, Celia Warren, not Ma, not caretaker, not antagonist, not loved and hated. Celia Warren was a pretty woman with curly hair she had given to Gwen. She was overweight and wore a sleeveless housecoat that both hid and exaggerated her weight. Her pale white arms that leaned on the table were delicately marbled with blue veins and Gwen always thought of them as the most perfect abstract art.

Gwen walked over, lifted the cigarette out of her mother's mouth, and put it out in the ashtray on the table. "I don't want to be an orphan before my time," Gwen said, moving to the stove and turning the heat on under the coffee.

Celia Warren never raised her eyes from the cookbook. "You can't be an orphan. Your father doesn't smoke. And anyway, Gwen, you know the wise saying 'You can't teach an old mother . . . ,' etc., etc."

Gwen poured a cup of coffee and sat down at the table.

"Make some toast or take some cereal or something. You have to be the health-nut type to make up for me."

"Not very hungry," Gwen said. "I'll pour some juice." She nodded in the direction of the cookbook. "What's all that about?"

Mrs. Warren looked up and smiled. "Your sister is coming for dinner and I thought it would be nice to make something special for her."

"How come Adrienne always gets the special meals and Dad and I keep getting meat loaf?"

"Gwen, stop it. That's just crazy and you know it."

Gwen shrugged and drank the strong, black coffee. "Is she bringing Davey with her?"

"No. She's leaving a one-year-old baby home by himself. It's time he learned to be independent . . . . Of course, she's bringing him."

"We, they could be getting a sitter. People don't always cart their kids everywhere they go."

Her mother looked at Gwen, knowing too much. "When the day comes that Adrienne and Joe can afford a sitter, I'll stand up and cheer."

"No one told her to get married at 18, and have a baby at 19. Unless she had to. Did she?" Gwen waited for her mother's answer.

"Why don't you ask *her*?"

"I have; she always says no."

Mrs. Warren laughed and looked down at the book again. "That's because it's true. She didn't *have* to get married. She fell in love with Joe and wanted to be his wife."

Gwen looked into her coffee cup, feeling the familiar self-disgust that made her slightly ill. She didn't mind being jealous of Adrienne, but to be jealous of a fairly cute one-year old boy, who just happened to be her nephew, was sick, sick, sick.

She stood up and put her cup in the dishwasher. Then she whirled around and said, "Hey, Ma, may I have the car? I want to go to the beach and just sit and watch the waves wave."

"It's too cold to go in the water. You do know that, right?"

"I won't go in, just look at it. Come on, say yes."

"Yes. But you'll have to stop at the market and pick up some things on your way back, and you have to be home by four. Deal?"

Gwen hugged her mother and kissed her shoulder. "Deal. You're not all bad, after all."

Gwen went up to her room, carefully made the bed, and put away the clothes she had worn the day before. She pulled some tissue from a box on the table and dusted the tops of the furniture. *Why,* she thought, *why do you do this? Why can't you just go and leave everything in a mess?*

"Yeah," she said out loud, making sure her door was closed. "Why don't you? You'd like to, so why do you have to be Miss Organized? Why can't you be more like Adrienne?"

Driving to the beach, Gwen thought about Adrienne. She had always been jealous of her. When Adrienne was treated seriously and with respect, *she* wanted to be treated that way. When Adrienne was teased, *she* wanted to be teased. She had inwardly seethed at any attention Adrienne got, as long as she could remember. The worst year had been the one when Adrienne had gone to college, before she dropped out to marry Joe Nadle. She had written long letters home, and Mrs. Warren had gathered together everyone who wasn't nailed down so that she could read the letters aloud. Gwen had always stormed out of the room and run up the stairs, to stand at the top silently and listen to the readings, because Adrienne really wasn't so bad . . . just always older, always ahead of wherever Gwen was.

Gwen slammed a fist on the steering wheel and said aloud, "You're a creep."

Then she became aware of the sound of the sea coming closer and the air becoming more moisture-filled and salty. The road had narrowed to two lanes and the greenery that edged it had given way to yellow-white sand and scrubby brush. There were fewer houses and those were weathered gray by the wind and water and salt.

She breathed deeply, feeling suddenly energetic and happy. She forgot about Adrienne and about Michael Abbott who had lived next door forever, who loved her and whom she didn't love. She forgot about the fight she had had the night before with her best friend, Manda Perlstein, about why Gwen didn't love Michael, whom Manda thought was great. All she was aware of now was that she was close to the sea, the water world she loved best.

She parked the car, carefully locking the doors, took off her shoes, tucked an old blanket and a tote under her arm, and trudged through the sand to a few yards from the water's edge. As she spread out the blanket, she could feel dampness under the surface of dry sand. It had rained the day before and only the top sand had dried. She dug her toes deep and let the coolness spread up her legs. Sitting on the blanket, she put her arms around her drawn-up legs and just watched the swirling ocean fling white whirls of water up onto the shore. Though the day was gentle, the sea was not and it crashed against the beach and withdrew wildly in an unceasing rhythm.

Suddenly, above the endless roll of the sea, she heard a girl screaming and laughing at the same time, "Stop it."

Gwen turned her head and saw a group of kids around the tall, deserted lifeguard stand. There were three boys and two girls, all in jeans and brightly colored T-shirts. One boy had a girl up in his arms and he was running toward the water with her, pretending he was about to toss her in. The girl kept yelling, "Stop," but obviously she was enjoying every minute of the ancient game. She both pummeled the boy's back and pushed him on toward the water at the same time. It was all a playful rite. The boy knew the girl wasn't really frightened and the girl knew the boy wasn't about to dump her in the water, but they went through the motions of terror and macho strength, each playing a role perfectly.

The other boy and girl were wrestling in the sand. Gwen smiled and then laughed out loud because the girl was obviously the stronger of the two and she quickly turned the boy on his back and held his arms at his sides. They were both startled by this unexpected turn of events, and the girl suddenly let go of the boy.

Then Gwen looked at the third boy, who was standing to the side, watching the others. He was part of the group but very much apart, all at the same time. Gwen looked away from him and then without willing it in any way she looked back. In all of her 16 years of life, she had never before experienced the sudden, unexplainable pounding of her heart at the sight of a boy or the need just to stare at a stranger.

She didn't even know what attracted her to him. He was only of medium height and wasn't well-built or athletic-looking. His hair was straight and sandy-colored yet he was too far away to tell what color his eyes were. But it was the way he moved to watch his friends; the way he turned his head with slow fluid movements that enchanted her. And it was also his very apartness from the four who were going through the never-changing beach play that linked her to him. Gwen and the boy were bonded by their separation from what was happening.

"Heavens," she breathed softly, and then just continued to stare at him, willing him to look her way.

He did. She couldn't tell if their eyes were meeting, but he was looking at her. Suddenly, Gwen was terribly embarrassed. She stretched out on her back and shut her eyes, letting the warmth of the sun ease the tension that had accumulated in every muscle and nerve in her body. She tried to breathe evenly and to return herself to the Gwen Warren who had come to the beach 20 minutes before. After all, she was sensible Gwen, steady Gwen. A cloud went over the sun blocking its warmth, and she opened her eyes.

But it *wasn't* a cloud that had come between her and the sun's heat. He was standing over her, staring down with a funny, sweet smile on his face. Now she knew. His eyes were an astounding amber color with darker gold flecks, and she stared unashamedly into them.

"Hi," he said easily.

"Hi," Gwen answered, sitting up and smiling nervously.

She wanted to pull her eyes away from his but couldn't.

"You were looking at me," he said, still smiling.

"I'm sorry," Gwen murmured, now distressingly embarrassed and uncomfortable. "I guess it was rude."

He shook his head and the dark-gold hair fell over his forehead. "No. I would have stared at you if I'd seen you first. Really."

He squatted down next to her in one easy, graceful movement. "I'm Jack O'Neal."

Gwen took a deep breath and looked away from him. "I'm Gwen." She hesitated and said nothing more.

Jack laughed. "I get it. You're Gwen no-last-name because your mother told you never to talk to strangers. Right?"

Gwen looked down at the sand and made little circles in it with her finger. "Something like that."

"Where do you live?" he asked suddenly.

Gwen hesitated again. "Seaview."

Jack looked at her carefully. "It's funny that I've never seen you around. I would have noticed you if I had."

Gwen felt her cheeks reddening and hated herself for it.

Jack leaned toward her. "Tell me everything about you."

Gwen laughed. "Well, I was born and . . ."

"I'm glad."

"Why? You don't know me. Why should you be glad I was born?"

Jack laughed softly, a wonderful laugh that Gwen heard all through her body. "Aha. *That* is where you are wrong. I know a lot about you. Just by looking at you."

Gwen narrowed her eyes, consciously flirting now. "Just what do you know?"

"Well, now, I know by looking at your eyes and hair and body that there is a career that was meant for you."

Gwen tried to look serious but she couldn't. "And what is that?"

"It's obvious. I see you in a tight, silver-spangled costume. You are high above an arena and about to do a death-defying stunt on the high trapeze. The audience is silent, waiting for Gwen the Great to begin. She takes a deep breath and swings over the crowd, does three somersaults to the opposite landing."

Gwen leaned forward and grabbed her knees, laughing loudly. "I don't think I'm the one you saw. Someone else, not me." But the idea that anyone pictured her in a silver-spangled costume overwhelmed her.

Jack shrugged. "All right. I see you as a glamorous spy. You are dressed all in black and have the secrets of many nations in your head."

"I feel sorry for our government if they're depending on me as a spy."

"Oh, no," Jack shouted. "You are above governments. It's not *our* country you spy for; it's for whoever pays you the most. You work for the highest bidder and the world bids for you because you're so good."

Gwen looked at this amazing boy and felt a kind of looseness, a freedom, emanating from him that she had never felt. Suddenly, he stood up and took her hand.

"Come on. Let's go in the water."

"You're crazy," Gwen said. "I don't even have a bathing suit with me."

"You have on shorts and a shirt. That's good enough." Jack pulled off his jeans; he had swimming trunks on under them. As he took off his shirt, he began running to the water. "Come on," he yelled again.

Gwen thought, *I told Mom I wouldn't go in*. She couldn't imagine Jack O'Neal's understanding that as any reason for not going into the water. Without actually knowing she was doing it, she ran after Jack. He jumped into the waves and Gwen followed him. The water was cold, too cold, but she didn't notice. They dove into the roaring waves and splashed water on each other and laughed and yelled and played.

After five minutes, Jack looked at her closely. "Your lips are getting blue. We'd better get out."

On the beach, Gwen wrapped her blanket around herself, but Jack just stood shaking the water off his body.

He bent down to Gwen. "OK, Gwen No-last-name who lives in Seaview, will you go out with me Friday night?"

Gwen looked at him in amazement. He was so unlike any of the boys she knew. He was totally at ease with the getting-to-know-you routine that most boys stumbled through and barely were able to articulate. Even Michael, whom she had known since she was seven, still had trouble making dates, setting up times and places and transportation. Jack O'Neal just went through it all as if he had done it a million times before. *And maybe he has,* Gwen thought with a sinking heart.

Gwen laughed out loud and pulled her knees up to her chin. "I can't go out with you. I don't even know you."

"So we'll get to know each other. Why can't you go to a movie with me?"

"OK," Gwen said, feeling suddenly defiant because she didn't like being put on the defensive. "*Can't* is the wrong word. I don't *want* to go out with you." *How you lie,* she thought. "You pick me up on the beach and you just assume I'm going to fall at your feet." *Which I almost did,* she realized.

Jack shrugged and stood up. "You can't live by all the dumb rules people make up."

"I don't," Gwen said angrily. "I live by *my* rules."

Jack brushed the sand off his hands. "Too bad," he said softly, and he reached down and touched her cheek gently. Then he walked away.

She turned her head so that she didn't have to watch him, but she could imagine the graceful movements of his body.

The sun had disappeared and with it the coming of summer. The sky was a metal gray and streaks of lavender bruised the horizon. Gwen shivered and put on her sweater, not looking at the group that was still laughing and shouting. She gathered up the blanket, her tote, and her shoes, and waded through the cold sand up the dunes at the top of the beach. Then she turned around and looked back to the lifeguard stand. Jack O'Neal was staring at her. She couldn't see the expression on his face, but she felt the funny, little smile. She raised her hand and waved at him slowly and he waved back. And then he turned away.

In the car, Gwen took off her wet T-shirt and put on her sweater. Pulling off the wet shorts, she put on a pair of jeans she had brought in the tote. She stuffed the wet clothes in the bag, hoping her mother wouldn't discover Gwen had been swimming. She ran her hands through her wet hair, but she knew, if she kept the car window open, her short hair would be dry by the time she got home.

She wondered why she had gone through all this for a boy she would never see again.

CHAPTER 2

Gwen drove back to Seaview, picked up the groceries her mother needed, and headed home, barely aware of what she was doing. She carefully avoided thinking about Jack O'Neal or the fact that she *was* avoiding thinking about him.

As she pulled into the driveway of the medium-sized, red-brick house in which she had lived in all her life, she saw Michael Abbott doing sit-ups on his front porch. She smiled as she watched him puff and pant. Jack O'Neal graceful, one-motion bending to squat next to her flashed before her and she rubbed her eyes. Suddenly she needed Michael's ordinariness, his peaceful boy-next-doorness. "Hey," she yelled.

Michael loped awkwardly over to her and opened the car door. He stepped back as Gwen got out and said, "Your mother said you went to the beach. Why didn't you tell me you were going? I would have come along."

Gwen shrugged. "I guess I just wanted to be alone for a little while. I'm sorry."

"It's OK. We'll be together tonight. Manda said we should come over there. Chuck's bringing over some new tapes. That all right with you?"

Gwen stared at Michael for a moment. She had totally forgotten they were double-dating with Chuck and Manda. How could she? It had become almost routine that she and Michael spent Friday and Saturday evenings together, but Manda would have a fit if she knew Gwen hadn't remembered they were all going to be together. It all seemed boring and predictable to her. How could the world be partly Chuck Wilson's tapes and partly Jack O'Neal's smile? How did they all fit into the same cosmic reality?

"Sure," Gwen reached out and patted Michael's shoulder. "It's OK. Pick me up at eight."

As she went into her house, she heard her mother and Adrienne laughing together and under the laughter, Davey's baby sounds and her father's cooing responses. They were the sounds of a family who were enjoying each other and Gwen felt left out and cold. She was aware of the familiar clutching in her stomach, knowing that somehow she was going to have to pretend sisterly feelings toward Adrienne.

Gwen felt like a jealous child, more childlike because she *knew* her negative feelings about Adrienne came from pure jealously. It was just that Gwen knew she could never do anything *first*. Adrienne always would have been there. If Gwen ever had a child, it would never be the *first* grandchild—Davey had already taken that position. No one would fuss over her maybe-to-be kid the way they did over Davey and over Adrienne because *she* had given birth to the *first* grandchild.

Adrienne will probably even die first, and everyone will crowd around her coffin, weeping and wailing. By the time I die, it will be old hat, Gwen thought.

All Gwen wanted to do now was escape into the shower, but first . . .

She walked to the entrance to the living room and said as happily as she could, "Hi, family."

Adrienne waved at her and smiled. "You've got a pink nose. The first of the season, lucky you."

Gwen smiled back at Adrienne and thought, *She's your sister. The only one you have . . . and she's really OK. You are just a creep.*

Adrienne was chubby, like their mother, with long dark hair and dark eyes. Since Davey had come along, her clothes were always not quite pressed, not quite clean. She was wearing jeans that were a little too tight and a red blouse that carried her badge of motherhood, Davey's lunchtime fingerprints. Gwen felt a moment of shock as she saw the blue shadows under Adrienne's eyes and the lines that faintly creased her forehead.

She turned away from Adrienne when she felt Davey's hands on her feet. He had crawled over to her and was looking up at her, trying hard to say who knew what. Gwen bent down and picked him up, resting her cheek against his head of feather-soft, bright blond curls. He immediately nestled against her and put his fingers in his mouth. Gwen held him tightly, loving him, and silently asking him to forgive her for not wanting him to be there.

Then she walked over to her father and handed Davey to him. "Be a grandfather. I have to take a shower."

She took a few steps and then turned back to her father. "Hey, Ethan, I thought accountants never left their offices in April until after the tax season was over. How did you make your getaway?"

Ethan Warren picked up a cup of coffee from the table near his favorite chair. "My name is Father, Dad, Daddy, Pops, Père, even Dadums to you. Take your choice. And I *just* left. When you have your own business, you risk starving to death, but you also can leave when you want."

"OK, Dadums. I'm glad you're here. I usually feel as if this is a one-parent home during tax time."

Gwen smiled at her father warmly and ran up to the bathroom. Under the shower, she held her face up to the warm water and let it rush down her cheeks and then roll down the rest of her body. She felt it wash away the sand and sweat of the beach and wished it could also wash away the memory of Jack O'Neal, whom she knew she would never see again.

Well, feet-on-the-ground Gwen, she thought. *Cool, logical Gwen. So cool, so logical that you know you'll make a super lawyer, what is with you?*

"What is with me," Gwen said aloud, knowing the closed door and running water would keep her secrets, "is that I have been bewitched by amber eyes and a funny smile. And since Jack is the prince, *who* can kiss me and remove his spell?"

Gwen turned off the water and wrapped a large white towel around herself. Then she sank to the floor of the bathroom and rocked back and forth.

Giving in to her strong need, she went over every minute of her encounter with Jack, remembering every movement, every tone of his voice and its changing rhythms, every blink of his eyes, every word. The ringing of the phone in her bedroom brought her back to the steamy bathroom. She ran into her room and swooped the phone off its hook. Her heart was racing even though she knew a boy who didn't even know her last name could not be calling her.

"Hi," Gwen said, trying to catch her breath.

"It's Manda. You sound as if you just finished a marathon."

"I was in the shower, I went to the beach and felt like a pail and shovel."

"Isn't it a little early for the beach?" Manda asked. "Was there anyone else there?"

For a moment Gwen yearned to tell her about Jack. She couldn't remember anything she had kept from Manda since they had met in second grade. Manda had fallen down a flight of stairs, taking Gwen, who had been unfortunate enough to be walking in front of Manda, with her. They hadn't been hurt but the togetherness of the rolling and tumbling down, down, down had formed a bond between them they had never broken.

Gwen hesitated. "Just a few kids playing teen-agers at the beach."

"I see it," Manda said. "Lots of wrestling and yelling and chasing each other around."

"On target," Gwen answered. Then, before she gave into the urge she knew she'd regret, she said, "Listen, I have to get dressed; Adrienne and Davey are here. I'll see you later."

— ♥ —

Joe Nadle arrived at six and the family sat down to dinner. Joe, always arrived on the dot when he was expected. One had no need for tides or moons or suns when Joe was around. He lived by routines, always predictable, always organized. Twenty-four years of living had made him cautious and careful, but the joy on his face when he looked at Adrienne was awesome and made up for a lot.

Dinner was like most family dinners. Everyone talked at once, passed endless dishes and platters of food, and watched Davey with admiration. He had just decided he could feed himself, but this was accomplished only with his fingers. His tiny hands shoveled everything into his mouth, including mashed potatoes and applesauce. Gwen's family thought this was a wonderful feat, but Gwen thought it was just disgusting and she left the table as quickly as possible, dropping a kiss on the top of Davey's head as she ran so that he wouldn't be insulted.

— ♥ —

The evening at Manda's was like innumerable ones before it. Chuck was a nice boy, similar to Michael in many ways, which was why they were close friends.

Manda was Manda. Beautiful as always with long, straight, dark-brown hair and big, brown eyes that expressed every emotion she felt, from the most fleeting to the deepest.

When she and Gwen were in the kitchen defrosting a

15

pizza, she gave Gwen a long look and then said, "I think you got too much sun today."

Gwen raised a hand to her pink nose and laughed. "Why is it always the nose that gets it?"

Manda shook her head. "That's not what I mean."

"What *do* you mean then?"

Manda perched on the edge of a heavy wooden table in the center of the kitchen and looked directly at Gwen. "I mean you're not with it tonight. It's as if you're someplace else. I can't reach you."

Gwen looked out of the kitchen window into blackness and then turned back to Manda. She was torn, wanting to keep Jack O'Neal to herself because it was all so ridiculous, and wanting to tell Manda about the alien, startling feelings she was having.

Gwen took a deep breath, held it, and then said swiftly, "I met a boy today."

Manda pushed herself off the table, her eyes wide and questioning.

Quickly Gwen told Manda about the beach and Jack and the breathless wild feelings she had had since she first saw him.

"You barely like any boy at all for 16 years and then you go crazy for a strange person you'll never see again. If you're looking for advice, kiddo, I certainly don't know what to tell you. I'm amazed. It's all so unlike my old friend Gwen."

Gwen laughed ruefully. "I know. But it's true."

"Have you ever seen him before? I mean, where do you suppose he goes to school?" Manda asked.

Gwen shrugged. "Who knows. He was a complete stranger to me and so were the other kids with him. They don't live in Seaview. That I know."

Manda put her arm around Gwen's shoulders and leaned her cheek against Gwen's for a moment. "Even if you never see him again, you've had an 'experience.' Chalk it up."

That night as Gwen lay in her bed, trying unsuccessfully to sleep, she thought about Manda's words. "Chalk it up." That seemed so final . . . and of course that was what her brief encounter with Jack was . . . final. Going nowhere. Zilch. But the faint salty smell of the sea that drifted into her room brought with it a memory of amber eyes.

CHAPTER 3

When Gwen left school on Monday afternoon, the promise of summer was gone. A cold, slanted rain poured down and tiny grains of hail pelted her face. She huddled down deep into her raincoat and pulled the hood as far over her forehead as she could. As she ran down the steps of Seaview High and toward the bus stop on the corner, a crash of thunder made her jump and the streak of lightning that followed dazzled her with its silvery spangles. *There never was a sun-struck beach and a boy with yellow eyes,* she thought.

"Gwen! Wait! Gwen!" A frantic voice cut through the rain and thunder. Gwen turned and watched Deirdre Zorro running toward her, waving and yelling, "Wait!"

Deirdre was in her gym class. They rarely said more than hello to each other and sometimes exchanged complaints about their martinet gym teacher whom they privately called the Sergeant. Gwen couldn't imagine what Deirdre would have to say that was so important that she would be racing after her in a rainstorm.

When Deirdre caught up with her, she tugged at Gwen's sleeve. "Come back with me, just for a minute."

"Back where?" Gwen asked, feeling annoyance as well as curiosity.

"Just to the side door. I have to talk to you." Because

18

Deirdr
her to t
When
was lean
He was w
up to him
Jack O'Nea
Then De
May I go no
Jack smiled,
wanted."
Deirdre loo
I've always sus
Gwen shivered
wildly by a heav
notice the loosen
way the turtlenec
men's-wear ad; and
don't really unders

turned the sand-colored hair to a dark cara
it to his head. Water dripped down
shoulders but he didn't seem to mi
seem to notice that he was gr
He was part of the rain, acc
Jack didn't wait for he
hand and started wa
"We'll go to D
you're freezi
Gwen
the s

a model in a
that still clung to hers. "I
don't really underst ly of this."

Deirdre wrapped her arms around herself to try to get warm. "Look, let *him* explain. I'm going home. You two may want to freeze standing here but I don't." She turned to Jack and said briefly, "You owe me one. OK?"

"Wait," Jack ordered. He took Gwen's arm and turned her to Deirdre. "Deirdre is my mother's best friend's daughter. We've known each other ever since, and all that. You know Deirdre; she knows me. Now you and I have been formally, legitimately, properly introduced. So properly that you can go out with me. Right?"

Deirdre left them standing in the rain as Gwen said, "It wasn't because we hadn't been 'formally' introduced. You make me sound like a character in a Jane Austen novel."

"Why then?" Jack asked.

Gwen looked at Jack and noticed for the first time that he didn't have on a jacket or anything on his head. The rain had

nel and plastered
his face and onto his
d. In fact, he didn't even
dually becoming drenched.
pting it, fusing with it.
to answer his question but took her
king, gently taking her along with him.
awson's for something hot. You look as if
g."
llowed along, no longer conscious of the wind or
aking rain. Her entire being was centered on the
rmth that came from the hand holding hers. She felt it travel up her arm, into her shoulder and neck, and spread into her brain.

Dawson's, the local high school coffee shop, was typical: noisy, crowded, and providing the kind of security you got at home, if you were lucky. It was almost empty that day and quiet, since most of the kids had been forced home by the storm.

Jack led Gwen to a booth and sat opposite her. He took a napkin from a holder on the table and wiped the rain off Gwen's face. She sat totally still as he did so, aware of every sound, every movement, every smell in the shop. It was a moment stopped in time for her . ... a forever. She saw Gloria, the waitress, wiping a table, her body arched as she bent over. She could smell coffee and hamburgers cooking and the cologne she had put on that morning. She heard the jukebox playing a country song by Alabama and she heard the rain beating against the windows. But most of all she was aware of Jack, of his hand on her face and the water still dripping from his head and his lips slightly parted as he finished patting her face dry.

Oh, Gwen, she thought, *what is happening to you? He's a stranger.*

"What would you like?" he asked.

She came back to the moment. "Um, tea, I guess."

Jack nodded. "What kind?"

"Kind?" Gwen repeated. "Just tea."

"Have you ever tried Earl Grey?" He rummaged in his backpack. "I have a box my mother asked me to buy for her. Try it."

Gloria came to the table and he said, "Just a cup of hot water for the lady. And I'll have coffee."

"Hot water?" Gloria asked. "Come on, Gwen. What's with you?"

Jack was unwrapping the box of tea he had and he held up a tea bag for Gloria to see. "She'll put this in the hot water."

Gloria shrugged and walked away.

"Are you hungry?" Jack asked. "Would you like something to eat?"

Gwen shook her head, thinking that Michael had never in his life asked her if she were hungry. If she just ordered tea, that was it. It never occurred to Michael to think she might want something more. Or maybe, if it were a day when he was paying, he just tried to save money. But Jack asked with ease. As if it were the most natural thing in the world to look after her in some almost paternal way.

When the hot water came, Jack put the Earl Grey tea bag in and swished it around until it was the strength he wanted.

"Now drink it."

Gwen took a sip and swallowed. It was delicious, with a smoky, heavy flavor that she had never tasted before. "It *is* good," she said. "I like it."

"I knew you would." He sat back and watched her as she drank the tea, pleased that he had pleased her. He lifted his coffee cup to his lips every few minutes, never taking his eyes from Gwen's face.

She put her cup down and asked, "What else do you like, besides Earl Grey tea?"

Jack leaned back in the booth, resting his head against its

back. "I only know what I like today. Tomorrow I may like something totally different. Things I hated yesterday, I like today."

"What do you like *today?*" Gwen asked. She was fishing; she knew it and she hated herself for it. Somehow Jack O'Neal had disturbed her knowledge of who she was. It excited Gwen and it frightened her. If she didn't know who Gwen Warren was, what were her guideposts? Where were her markers?

Jack smiled. "What do I like today? I like that waitress pretending she's what's-her-name on that TV program, "Alice." You know . . . Flo. Look at Gloria, with the pencil behind her ear and that silly, huge, artificial flower pinned to her uniform. She knows she's playing a game and I like that. I like the way the coffee tastes, bitter and not fresh. I like the smells in here, wet raincoats and spilled ketchup and your perfume. And I like the rain banging against the window."

Gwen felt a rush of emotion that startled her. His answer wasn't what she had wanted and she felt close to tears of humiliation and disappointment. She looked away for a moment and then back at Jack and smiled, as if his answer had been just what she had expected.

Then he leaned toward her and took her hand. "And I like you. And being here with you and knowing we are just beginning."

"Beginning what?" Gwen asked, never taking her eyes from him.

Jack shrugged. "Does it matter? Do we have to know right now what is beginning?"

Gwen did. That was the kind of girl she was; she always wanted to know where she had been and was and was going. But now with Jack O'Neal looking at her with a soft, sweet gaze, she said, "No, of course not."

If he knew, she wondered, if he knew that she needed the security of *knowing* what was beginning, would he still be interested in her? She was afraid the truth would end whatever feelings he had for her.

Gwen laughed. "Well, if you don't know what's beginning, can you at least tell me where you live? What your family is like? Common-knowledge stuff like that."

"That much I do know," he said. "I live in Westside. Convenient for us, yes? A quick ten miles from Seaview. My father is a salesman and we're really pals, do things together. We're alike. My mother is a substitute teacher. We're not alike. I'm the only kid and I like the attention. I shouldn't tell you that. You'll think I'm a spoiled brat . . . and I'm not. Now you. You live in Seaview . . . and . . .?"

Gwen took a deep breath. "I live in Seaview. My father is an accountant. We don't pal around; he's Dad." (Dadums, she thought, smiling to herself) "My mother is a housewife. I have an older sister, Adrienne. She's married and has a year-old baby."

Gwen had been stirring her tea as she spoke, not looking at Jack. When she raised her eyes to his, she knew he had been listening totally, intensely. As if everything about her were important. No one had ever been that interested in her family tree before. No one had ever been that riveted by her. It was flattering, it drew her to him even more than his amber eyes and grace and Earl Grey tea. *He wouldn't be impressed by Adrienne,* she thought.

"Do you like them? Your parents? Your sister?"

"They're OK." She wasn't ready to talk about Adrienne to him. She was afraid he wouldn't understand . . . yet.

Suddenly he looked at his watch. "Geez. I've got to go. I told Mom I'd be home an hour ago to drive her to the dentist. Her car is in the shop and I've got mine with me."

"That's impressive," Gwen said. "You have your own car?"

"Don't be impressed until you see it," Jack said. "It's an old heap I fixed up. It runs, but just."

He reached over and helped her put on her raincoat, his

23

hand brushing her cheek as he did. "Let's go to a movie tomorrow night? OK?"

Gwen hesitated, reluctant to answer. "I . . . I can't. I mean, I don't date on week nights."

Jack smiled that funny smile. "More rules? You can't go out on school nights?"

When he saw her eyes darken, he reached over and stroked her cheek. "It's OK. Really. Don't look like that."

She wondered how someone that attractive to her could make her so angry, so on edge. "It isn't that my mother locks me in my room Monday through Thursday. It's just . . . it's just that she'd rather I didn't go out. And it's OK with me. I've always got a lot of work to do and I've got to get high grades if I want to . . ."

She'd been about to tell him she eventually had to get into law school, but what would being a lawyer seem to someone as mercurial as Jack O'Neal? She didn't finish the sentence.

"Please," he said softly. "Don't be angry. How about Friday night?"

Gwen felt the anger leave as suddenly as it had come. "Friday is fine."

They left the coffee shop holding hands.

His thumb stroked the inside of her wrist and she knew he had to feel the heightened beat of her pulse. All of Michael's kisses had never made her soar the way this gentle movement on her wrist did.

It was still raining and Gwen pulled Jack's turtleneck sweater up higher on his throat. But Jack didn't seem to notice the driving torrents. They stood and looked into each other's eyes, barely breathing.

"I'll drive you home. My car is in the lot," he finally said.

"No. You're late as it is. My bus is right on the corner. I'll be fine."

"Sure?" he asked.

"Sure."

He bent forward and brushed her cheek with his lips. "I'll call you about Friday." Then, as he had done on the beach, he turned quickly and walked away. She stared after him and then ran to the bus.

CHAPTER 4

Once she was seated in the bus, she knew she couldn't go home. She felt too disoriented, too excited to face the dull routine of her house. When the bus stopped on Manda's corner, Gwen got off and slowly walked down the street to Manda's small white house.

The door was unlocked, as always, and Gwen went in, calling out, "Manda?"

Manda's mother was a writer and at Gwen's shout she opened her studio door and leaned against it. "Distract me."

Gwen looked at Vivian Perlstein admiringly and smiled. She was a tall woman with bright blonde hair that was pulled back into a ponytail. She had on old jeans and a large sweat shirt that couldn't hide her slim elegance.

"Why do you want to be distracted?" Gwen asked.

"Because I'm tired of writing historical romances. I have nothing romantic to say today. Maybe I'll never have anything to say."

Gwen didn't know how to answer that but she didn't feel uncomfortable. Vivian Perlstein never made her feel she expected any helpful answers. All she wanted was an ear.

Mrs. Perlstein waved at Gwen. "Manda is upstairs. Tell her there is a brand-new, uncut, just-bought cake in the kitchen, full of additives and preservatives. You'll love it."

Manda's room was like Manda, eclectic. There were stark Swedish bookcases; a Victorian brass bed; an old, falling-apart, velvet armchair; and a small French desk. The walls were covered with modern prints, posters, Renaissance drawings, and bright Edward Hopper reproductions. There were pillows on the bed and the floor and on the chair. At that moment, Manda was sitting on the floor, leaning against the gold velvet chair, reading Anne Sexton's poetry.

Manda looked up as Gwen walked into the room, leaving a trail of water behind her. Gwen stood silently, dripping small, dull raindrops.

"I didn't expect you," Manda said. "You OK?"

Gwen hovered over Manda, not knowing exactly why she was there.

Manda moved slightly and wiped her face with the back of her hand. "Do you mind dripping somewhere else?"

Gwen sank down to the floor and mumbled, "Sorry." Then she nodded her head in the direction of Manda's book. "How can you read such depressing stuff?"

"It's not *all* depressing. Just because she wound up killing herself doesn't mean she only wrote painful poems. But did you come here to discuss Anne Sexton?"

Gwen stretched out on her back and stared up at the ceiling. "I don't know why I'm here. I just couldn't go home. I feel too weird."

"There's a lot of flu around so don't breathe on me."

Gwen sat up abruptly. "I don't mean that kind of weird. I mean emotionally weird." Her voice broke slightly and Manda caught the tremor immediately.

"Why?" Manda asked with concern. "I mean did anything happen today to upset you?"

Gwen got up and walked over to the window. She looked out at the slate rain and said, "I saw Jack O'Neal today. He found out who I was, met me at school, and took me out for tea."

Manda didn't move. "And?" she asked.

Gwen spun around and said angrily, "And? And I feel nauseous and like crying."

"That's love," Manda said. "I always throw up the first week I'm in love."

Gwen sat down again and stared at the floor. "How can I be in love with a boy I barely know? It doesn't make sense."

Manda was suddenly totally serious. "Gwennie, everything that happens to a person doesn't always make sense. *You* just expect it to. What's so senseless anyway? You see a guy on the beach . . . he's attractive . . . and you find out he's bright, funny, different. Then he even makes an effort to find you. It's exciting. It's like what you read in romance novels. My mother writes about it all the time. Why *shouldn't* you fall in love with him? I think I'm in love with him myself."

Gwen smiled at Manda. Manda was always so *herself*. She managed to push away all the confusion and come out Manda.

"You know what *really* bothers me? Not why *I'm* attracted to him, but why is *he* interested in me? He's magical and I'm so earthbound. He seems so spontaneous and I'm so routinized. Why does he want to be with me? Maybe he's just teasing."

Manda reached over and brushed some of the rain out of Gwen's hair. "Maybe he likes your solidity and directness. You've only spent about an hour with each other. How can either of you know what and why yet?"

"That's what *he* said . . . almost."

"I think what's happened is great for you. It will lighten you up a little. It will make you more adolescent . . . as the books say we should be. It's time for you, Gwennie."

Gwen laughed. "You're a romantic, Manda."

Manda looked away for a moment and then back at Gwen. "No, Gwen, that's not true. You can't believe much in forever after when your mother and father split after having been married 20 years. Deep down, I'm just as realistic as you are."

"I've never heard you say anything like that before."

"I've said it, Gwen . . . in different ways. You haven't heard."

"I get so wound up in my own needs and plans and feelings, maybe sometimes I don't listen." Gwen looked at her watch and said with regret, "I've got to go home. It's getting late."

"Stay for dinner," Manda said. "Mom will love it. She'd probably rather have dinner with you than me any day."

Gwen hesitated. "What are you having?"

"Spaghetti, I think," Manda answered, going back to her book.

"From the can?"

Manda looked up. "No, Mom and I made the sauce last night. It even looks edible."

Gwen said dubiously, "I'm not sure what is worse, the stuff in the can or what you and your mother cook. But I'll stay anyway."

"Gee, thanks. You're so gracious," Manda said, smiling. "Call your mom so she doesn't think you've been kidnapped or run over or something."

Gwen always enjoyed dinner at the Perlsteins. Her own house was casual, but Vivian Perlstein's was casual to the point of chaos. Since 75 percent of her mind was always on the book she was writing, it was an accident if there happened to be enough paper napkins and clean dishes. But the conversation was always interesting and made up for the haphazard food.

Gwen tasted the spaghetti warily and then said with surprise, "It's not bad. Almost decent."

Vivian Perlstein stopped eating, her fork raised toward her mouth. "I guess I'm a lousy mother in the household department. There's never enough time. I'm always late for something . . . a deadline . . . a dinner . . . something."

"You're OK," Manda said, "not perfect, but OK."

Vivian nodded. "Yeah, I guess so. I know the important things . . . like you're not doing drugs; you do OK at school; you're healthy. What more can I ask for?"

"What about dating?" Manda said, teasing. "You have no idea what I'm doing in that department."

Gwen looked at Manda with surprise since she knew Manda wasn't doing anything much in that department.

Vivian shook her head and held up her hand. "Confide in Gwen when it comes to dating. I've taught you all I know. Now you have to use your common sense and clear head and your knowledge of what's good for you and what isn't. I hope you know."

Gwen liked Vivian's attitude. Her own mother was more involved, asking what she thought were discreet questions about what Gwen and Michael were doing. Gwen knew her mother thought she was being subtle but she was really as heavy-handed as she could be without coming right out and asking, "What do you do on your dates?"

After coffee, Manda's mother got up and stretched. "I've got to get back to Henry VIII and Anne Boleyn. You kids will have to clean up."

"How can you be so interested in those two? You know how it ends . . . he's going to lop her head off," Manda said, clearing the table.

"Yes, but our heroine, the beautiful, violet-eyed, Edena, doesn't know. I can hardly wait to finish the book and dump Edena."

"I don't see how you do it," Gwen said. "One after another like that."

Vivian shrugged. "Well, it keeps the food on the table. Something Manda's father isn't about to do."

When Vivian saw the look of pain that crossed Manda's

face, she said, "I'm sorry, honey. I don't mean to be nasty about him. I know you love him."

Manda didn't answer.

———♥———

Later when Gwen was walking home, she wondered what it would be like to be married to someone for 20 years and then end up hating him. Her parents were still so close, so together, that it was hard to imagine.

The rain had stopped but the budded branches of the trees lining the streets dripped cold drops. The air was soft and sea-filled, wrapping Gwen in a cool cottony coat. The streets were quiet except for the occasional barking of a dog or the blast of a stereo before it was turned down. Gwen held her face up to the sky and stood with her eyes closed. Suddenly Jack was very close again. The smell, the feel, the wetness of the air took her back to the beach and the endless ocean. A silver wave of joy washed over Gwen and she gave herself up to it completely, letting it spill over her.

Her mother and father were in the living room when Gwen went into the house. Her mother was reading and her father was working on tax reports.

"Have a good dinner?" Celia Warren asked.

"Pretty good for the Perlsteins. It hasn't come up yet."

Ethan Warren looked at Gwen from under thick eyebrows. "Well, Vivian might be a terrible cook but she's a very good-looking woman."

Celia looked at her husband with surprise and unconsciously her hand went up to smooth her hair. Gwen giggled to herself at her mother's reaction.

"You can look but don't touch," Mrs. Warren said warily.

Ethan Warren smiled at his wife warmly. "Not to worry."

The calm affection drifting between her mother and father touched Gwen, but it was so different from the wave of feeling she had just had for Jack O'Neal that she couldn't believe they both sprang from affection of any similar kind.

She waved at her parents. "Me for bed."

In her room, she undressed quickly, not bothering to brush her teeth or wash her face. She slipped into bed and lay on her back, gazing at the ceiling. The house was totally still and she could almost hear her heart beating and her blood flowing through her body. Her ears rang slightly in the silence as she tried to recapture the sound of Jack's voice.

Suddenly she got up, turned on the light, and reached for the telephone book that was on the shelf under the table that held the phone. She leafed through the pages until she came to the listings for Westside. Hunting for a listing for O'Neal, she finally found just one: Ira O'Neal; 241 Center Street; 476-9088. Gwen stared at the number and then carefully wrote it in her address book.

Jack assumed a reality now that he hadn't had before. His father's name was Ira. He lived on Center Street and his phone number was neatly printed in her address book. He existed. As Gwen fell asleep, she thought with panic, *Supposing that weren't Jack's address? Supposing it were a different O'Neal?*

— ♥ —

Gwen felt she'd only slept a few minutes when the ringing of the phone pierced the darkness. She sat up with a jolt and peered at the glow-in-the-dark clock on her night table. It was just midnight. Gwen fumbled for the phone and said, still half asleep, "'Lo."

"Did I wake you?" Jack's soft voice brought Gwen to total awareness.

"Well, yes. But it's OK." *Why did you say you'd been asleep?* she thought. *Why didn't you let him think you were up painting your toenails purple or somethig equally exotic?*

"I just wanted to tell you I'm thinking about you."

Gwen tried to focus entirely on Jack's words and not think

about whether the ringing phone had wakened her parents. His voice was silky and deeper on the phone than in person.

"I've been thinking about you too," Gwen said, sinking back down under the covers and closing her eyes. She felt warm and aware of the beating of her heart.

"I'm glad," Jack whispered. "I'll talk to you soon."

Gwen sat upright again. "Wait," she cried out.

"I'm here."

Gwen clutched the phone. "Is your father's name Ira and do you live on Center Street?"

Jack laughed and answered, "Yes. Why?"

"Just wanted to know." Gwen felt embarrassed and couldn't tell Jack that she had his number in her phone book and that it was crucial to her that it be there.

"Good night, Jack." Gwen hung up and, wrapping the blankets tightly around her, curled into a small ball of girl. The room was filled with Jack. The softness and exciting warmth of his voice was in the corners and spilling across the floor and covering the ceiling. Gwen closed her eyes but it was a long time before she fell asleep.

CHAPTER 5

When Gwen went downstairs for breakfast, her mother and father were almost through eating. Mr. Warren looked up from his newspaper and asked, "Did you get a phone call about midnight last night?"

Gwen was silent for a moment. How could she tell them it was from Jack when they didn't even know he existed? And how would they react to a midnight caller? Before she knew what she was doing, she heard herself say, "It was a wrong number. I didn't think you'd hear it since my door was closed."

Gwen's mother bit a piece of toast and chewed thoughtfully. "Who would call anyone in the middle of the night unless it were an emergency?"

Gwen suddenly felt hemmed in, as if the room were slowly getting smaller and smaller. *That's* how they'd react to a midnight caller. "You know, there *are* people who don't think that 12 o'clock is the middle of the night. Everyone doesn't go to bed early." She was surprised at how irritated she sounded, how sharp her voice was.

Gwen's father didn't answer but Celia Warren said, "What's all the excitement about? You'd think we were bad-mouthing someone you knew."

Exactly, thought Gwen. Aloud she said, "I have to run.

I'm late for a change." She finished her orange juice as she stood up and ran out of the kitchen, grabbing her books, a jacket, and her violin from the foyer bench.

As she walked to the bus stop, she thought, *When was the last time you lied to your parents? And why did you now? It was a dumb, childish thing, not even worthy of being called a lie. Lies should be big. Lies should be important. You really are a jerk.*

On the bus she remembered that when she was ten, she went through a few weeks of going through her mother's pocketbook every few days and taking all the loose change. While Mrs. Warren never asked Gwen if she were stealing the money, Gwen considered that the last time she had deliberately lied to her mother.

Gwen shifted the violin case and rested her chin on it. She had been playing the violin for two years and went for one lesson a week. She wasn't very good but she enjoyed the feelings of peace and accomplishment she had when she played. She never practiced enough to make any dramatic improvement but the Tuesday afternoon lessons were a time of separateness for her. She was away from her family, from friends, from Michael.

Michael, she thought suddenly and almost leaped up from the bus seat. They saw each other every Friday and Saturday night. It was a quiet expectation they had of each other. At least it was quiet for her. She knew Michael felt differently, that he cared about her in a way she had never been able to match.

When Manda got on the bus a few stops later, Gwen waved to her wildly. Manda sank into the seat next to Gwen and took out her comb, pushing it through her long, tangled hair.

"Nothing like getting up with just enough time to put on your clothes. I haven't even washed my face." She opened her tote and motioned to a toothbrush and paste. "Think anyone will mind if I brush here?" She smiled at what she considered her own hilarity.

"What am I going to tell Michael about Friday night?" Gwen asked, ignoring Manda's dental problems.

"I don't know. I mean, if you're honest and tell him about Jack, he's going to be mad and you can't blame him. Maybe you shouldn't mention Jack. For all you know, you may never see him again after Friday. You may *hate* being with him."

Gwen stared out of the window. *I'm going to love being with him,* she thought. *Love it.*

"If you have to make up some story or other, you can use me as an excuse. Tell him you have to help me study or something."

Gwen twisted in her seat, feeling a kind of inner discomfort that was unfamiliar to her. "I lied to my parents this morning. I told them it was a wrong number on the phone at midnight when it was Jack. I don't want to lie to Michael too."

"He called at midnight?" Manda asked "Why?"

Gwen took the comb that now was stuck in Manda's hair and started trying to get it loose. "He's not like most other people, Manda. He doesn't care if it's 7 or 8 or 12. If he wants to call, he calls."

"You should introduce him to my mother. She's up half the night working anyway. They could have long, philosophical discussions while the rest of us peasants sleep."

Gwen laughed. "My father already thinks your mother is a good-looking woman. I don't need Jack thinking that too."

"No kidding," Manda said. "I wouldn't mind having your dad as a father; maybe I'll tell my mom to change accountants."

Gwen punched Manda's arm. "You're nuts."

When Gwen came out of school at three, the sun was cascading over the school grounds, shooting golden rays over the still-brown earth and the barren trees. She hoisted her violin under her arm as she tried to get her bus pass from her tote. Suddenly she felt the violin being taken from her. She spun around and faced Jack, who was holding the violin case and smiling.

"Come on. We'll buy some food and go down to the beach for a picnic."

They stood facing each other silently, her eyes caught by what was reflected in his. He put his free arm around her shoulders and she felt the warmth of his hand through her jacket and sweater. She bent her head and rested her cheek against his hand for one small, shattering moment.

As she lifted her head, she said, "I can't. I have a violin lesson, the proof being the violin you're holding."

"It's too great a day to be inside playing a violin. Call your teacher and tell her you can't come. Tell her the sun calls and you have to follow."

Gwen wanted to go with Jack with every cell in her body, but the desperate wanting held her back. If she gave in now, she felt she would be lost forever.

"I can't. I mean I *want* to go for my lesson. I like them."

"Do you want the lesson more than you want to be with me at the beach?"

Gwen felt trapped and she turned away, looking for a place to run. Then she faced Jack again. "No, not more. I want both but I have lessons on Tuesday and I have to go."

She touched Jack's arm gently. "How about tomorrow? We can go to the beach tomorrow, can't we?"

Jack picked up an end of his long blue scarf and threw it around his neck with a gesture that stopped Gwen's breath. "Tomorrow is too far away to plan. Tomorrow it may rain or snow or it may never come."

Gwen felt tears come to her eyes but she blinked them back. Then Jack hugged her and guided her to the parking lot. "Come on, I'll drive you to this irresistible lesson. I never thought I'd play second fiddle to a violin." He winked at his ridiculous joke and they both laughed, breaking the painful tension.

When Gwen got out of the car, she asked fearfully, "I'll see you Friday?"

"Without a doubt. Call you."

That night as Gwen lay in bed, she knew she was waiting . . . waiting for the phone to ring. Stillness lay over the room like a gray quilt of fog.

Maybe he's angry, she thought. *Why didn't I just call Miss Branfer and cancel the violin lesson? What was so important about it?*

What was so important, she answered herself, *is that you like the lessons . . . and Miss Branfer expected you. It was a commitment.*

Big deal, can't I ever uncommit?

Yes, you can, when you want to. Did you want to?

I wanted both. I wanted to go with Jack and to take the lesson. Can't I have both?

Sure you can have both. Just stay calm.

Maybe he'll never call again. Maybe he feels rejected.

Oh, for heaven's sake, go to sleep.

Gwen smiled in the dark and closed her eyes.

—— ♥ ——

Every day after school, Gwen looked out of the corners of her eyes for Jack, trying to pretend she wasn't looking. Every night she waited for the phone to ring. Finally on Thursday night, he called, and a feeling of relief washed over her.

"How about a movie tomorrow night?" he asked.

"Fine," Gwen twisted the phone cord as she spoke. "What time?"

"Well, do you like foreign films?"

"I haven't seen too many but, sure, I like them."

"OK, there's a good Italian movie in Beachwood. It goes on at eight, so I'll pick you up at seven . . . Gwen . . . I can't wait to see you again."

Gwen's toes curled as he spoke. "Me too."

As she hung up the phone, a feeling of guilt and panic replaced the one of relief. Frantically she dialed Manda's number.

As soon as Gwen heard Manda's voice, she began to talk. "Listen, Jack just called and I am going to see him tomorrow night and I haven't told Michael anything and I don't know what to tell him and what should I do?"

"For a girl who plans ahead, Gwen, you sure waited until the last minute to handle this little item."

"I was afraid Jack wouldn't call, so I thought why . . ."

Manda sighed. "Why rock your boat with Michael, eh?"

"That sounds so awful. Manda, I'm a crumb."

"To a degree. You just wanted to cover all your bases, girl. That's human."

"Maybe human, but it doesn't make me like me very much."

"Gwen, stop agonizing. Call Michael this minute and tell him *something*. This minute!"

"OK, OK."

Gwen hung up and tried to think of what to say to Michael. Michael was dear to her, important to her. They had been friends since he had moved next door. Then friendship had turned to other things . . . love for Michael . . . and something hard to characterize for Gwen. She loved him in a quiet, gentle way. He comforted her when she needed comforting; encouraged her when she needed encouraging; was her steady date, ensuring her entry into all the social life of Seaview. And he seemed not too aware that their kisses and caresses were not as thrilling to Gwen as they were to him.

Gwen knew she had two choices: she could lie to Michael

now or she could tell the truth. As she dialed his number, she had no idea which way she was going.

Michael anwered the phone and Gwen plunged ahead. "Michael, listen, about tomorrow night . . ."

"I thought maybe we could go to a movie," Michael said.

An Italian one? Gwen thought and almost giggled.

"No, listen, something's come up. There's this kid in school, Deirdre Zorro, and she had a date with this guy who's her mother's best friend's son and she met this boy she's crazy about and she doesn't want her mother to know she isn't going to see this best friend's son and so in gym the other day she asked me, begged me, if just this once I'd go out with this best friend's son so that she didn't feel so guilty. I mean she cried and carried on and before I knew what I was doing I said yes, just to shut her up. It was awful, Michael, you would have done the same thing. I know it."

Michael was silent. Then he said, "Let me get this straight. You're saying you're not going to see me tomorrow night; you have another date."

Gwen felt embarrassment start crawling up from her toes to the curl hanging on her forehead. Words tapped in her head. *There was a little girl, who had a little curl, right in the middle of her forehead. And when she was good, she was very, very good, and when she was bad she was horrid.*

"Michael, it isn't really a date. It's just a nothing, Just a . . ."

"Gwen, you hardly know this Deirdre Zorro girl. Why do you have to do her a favor at my expense?"

"I'm sorry, Michael. I just didn't think." Gwen felt a tear begin to wander slowly, slowly, down her cheek. *You're a louse*, she thought. *A real louse.* She felt shame and remorse, but no lessening of her determination to see Jack O'Neal.

"What's his name?"

"Whose name?"

"The guy," Michael shouted. "The guy you're going to date?"

"It's Jack . . . Jack O'Neal."

"Never heard of him."

"He doesn't live in Seaview. He lives in Westside."

"Can't he find a girl in Westside?" Michael's voice was deep with anger and confusion.

"Oh, I don't know. I didn't ask. She just begged and I said OK." Gwen was almost believing the story now. *That Deirdre always was a whiner,* she thought.

"You always were an easy mark for anyone in trouble." Michael's voice was softer, relenting. "OK, it's just one night. Just don't do it again, Gwen."

"Sure, Mike, sure. It won't happen again." *But you know it will if Jack asks again. Michael, I'm sorry,* she thought to herself, *I am.*

CHAPTER *6*

In the morning as Gwen came into the kitchen for breakfast, she realized she had to say something to her parents about her date that night. She couldn't just wait until Jack arrived.

As she poured cold cereal into a bowl, she said quickly and with as much confidence as she could muster, "Listen, I have a date with a guy tonight . . . and it isn't Michael."

Celia and Ethan Warren both looked up from their breakfast at the same moment. "Who is he?" Gwen's mother asked.

"It's a boy I met at the beach." Gwen put a spoonful of cereal in her mouth, hoping she wouldn't have to add to what she'd said.

Her father drew his thick eyebrows together and waited for Gwen to say something more. When she didn't, he asked, "*How* did you meet him at the beach?"

Gwen knew then that Ethan Warren was not going to be very happy about his daughter going out with a guy who had just picked her up because she had been giving him the eye. She took a deep breath.

"What do you mean how? I met him at the beach. Deirdre Zorro, a kid in my gym class, introduced us. He's her mother's best friend's son."

That's not a lie, Gwen thought. *I did meet him at the beach and Deirdre did introduce us*. The order of things was just a little mixed.

Mr. Warren relaxed. "Oh, well, that sounds OK. For a minute I thought some creep just picked you up."

Celia Warren pushed her hair back from her forehead and looked at Gwen quizzically. "What about Michael? What did you tell him? Or didn't you tell him?"

"Of course I told him," Gwen said with a superior tone.

"And it was OK with him?" Mrs. Warren persisted.

"Well, he wasn't exactly delighted but . . . he understood."

This is awful, Gwen thought. *I don't even know what I'm saying any more*.

"He's a bigger man than I would have been at his age," Mr. Warren said. "But I can't say I mind your seeing other guys. You're too young to date just one boy."

Gwen jumped up from the table, frantic to get away. "I have to go." She dropped a kiss on the top of her mother's head and ran from the kitchen.

By six o'clock on Friday, Gwen had eaten a quick sandwich, showered, washed her hair, and was standing looking at the chaos in her bedroom. There were clothes everywhere. Jeans, skirts, blouses, sweaters: pink, red, green, yellow, blue. She wanted to look gorgeous and casual. Unforgettable and laid back. Now she stood helplessly, not knowing what to pull from the heaps of things on the bed and floor. Suddenly she was aware of someone behind her and she turned to face Adrienne.

Adrienne was looking at the array of clothes wistfully. She self-consciously raised her hand to a split in the seam of the T-shirt she was wearing and fruitlessly tried to pull it together. Then she walked over the bed and picked up a soft, loose, pink sweater.

"Nice," she said softly.

"I didn't know you were coming over," Gwen said.

"Mom is baby-sitting for Davey. Joe and I are going for a pizza . . . big Friday night doings."

Gwen turned away, not wanting to tune in on Adrienne's feelings. Not wanting to understand or empathize with her. *Go away*, she thought. *Let me get ready for Jack without your looking like Cinderella.*

"Big date with Michael?" Adrienne asked.

"No. Just a guy I'm seeing as a favor to a friend."

"Sounds nice anyway. Something different. Life should have *some* different things in it. Some things you can't predict."

Adrienne ran down the stairs and Gwen stared after her for a moment. Was Adrienne jealous of *her*? Couldn't be.

Gwen straightened her shoulders and with determination she pulled a pair of slim jeans from a pile and picked up the pink sweater. She put them on, checking off the way her long legs and small, curved rear looked in the tight jeans, and how the loose sweater both concealed and emphasized her trim body and small shoulders. She brushed her hair until it waved wildly around her face, outlined her eyes, and put a moist layer of pink gloss on her lips. She grabbed a wool jacket from her closet and went down into the living room.

At seven she heard Jack's car and raced out of the house. Her mother's voice trailed behind her, "Gwen, have the boy come in. We want to meet . . ."

No, Gwen was thinking. *Not tonight. Not tonight.*

She opened the door to Jack's car and moved into the seat beside him, smiling at him as she settled down.

"Hey! Are you ashamed of me or something? I usually come into a girl's house, meet her parents, charm them, and reassure them that I'll drive carefully and get her back home in one piece."

Gwen laughed. "Of course I'm not ashamed of you. I thought we might be late for the movie if my parents got you into some long conversation."

Silently she was mulling over how many girls' houses he visited and how many parents he had charmed. *No! I won't spoil tonight. I won't. I'm the one he's with tonight.*

Jack turned to her in the dark and gave her a quick look. "Pretty. More than pretty, beautiful."

Gwen felt a flush steal over her face. No boy had ever told her she was beautiful before. It was wonderful and she let herself believe it. In the lights of passing cars, she saw Jack's blond hair was still wet from a shower and it threw off silver shots like a sparkler. She smelled the faint odor of tangy after-shave lotion and she breathed it in deeply, leaning her head against the seat as she did. She wanted to reach over and touch his hand or his cheek or his knee. She clasped her fingers together tightly so that she didn't. Then he reached over and gently ran his fingers down her cheek. She closed her eyes.

He turned into the theater's parking lot and stopped the car with a jolt. Gwen sprang forward in the seat and clutched the dashboard.

"Sorry about that," Jack said, smiling his wondrous smile. He got out of the car and sped around to open the door for her, bowing as she got out. Unable to resist another moment, she put her hand out and touched his damp hair.

When they got to the box office, Gwen reached into her bag for the money for her ticket. Jack shook his head. "Not tonight. First date is on me. No arguments. You can pay when we fly to Paris."

Gwen moved away from the box-office line and looked at the advertisements for the movie. Under the title she read in small black letters, NO SUBTITLES. She turned frantically to Jack before he bought the tickets but he was suddenly at her side, holding two pink tickets.

"I don't speak Italian. I don't understand it . . . not a word," Gwen said. "I mean, I won't know a thing that's going on."

Jack grinned. "I don't speak Italian either. You don't have to."

"But of course you have to if you want to follow the movie."

Jack put a hand on her arm and steered her into the theater. "No. If the actors are good, you'll know what's happening just by their movements and expressions . . . by their body language. You'll see, I'm right."

Want to bet, Gwen thought.

As they passed the popcorn counter, Gwen stared longingly at the greasy yellow corn. Obviously popcorn was not appropriate at an Italian movie with no subtitles.

The movie began as soon as they sat down. *Il Scandalo*.

Jack leaned over. "*The Scandal*, that much I understand."

Gwen sighed softly. She was ahead. At least she knew what the title of the movie was. She relaxed a little. Then she was aware of Jack's breathing softly next to her, of his shoulder's touching hers, and his knee an inch away. He reached for her hand and held it loosely. She was sure he must be aware of the quickening of her breath. She leaned toward him slightly. Then she tried to concentrate on the screen.

People moved. Talked. Laughed. There seemed to be three men and a woman who were causing the scandal. There was anger. Tears. And finally a shooting. But in reality Gwen hardly knew what was happening. To complicate things further, two of the men had dark hair and mustaches and looked almost alike to Gwen.

It was one of those movies that depended on inner feelings rather than action, and Gwen found that she soon lost track of who was doing what to whom . . . and she didn't care much. Jack, on the other hand, was lost in the picture. He laughed in the right places, wiped a tear away at one point, and leaned forward intently when the two men were talking endlessly.

Gwen concentrated on Jack and forgot about the movie. She listened to his staccato laugh. She watched the way his body moved when he shifted in his seat and leaned one way or the other. She even marveled at the way he blew his nose. When the movie was over and they walked out into the crisp night, Jack took her hand again.

"Wasn't I right? Didn't you understand most of it?" As he talked, he guided her across the street to a big pizza restaurant. "Do you like pizza?"

"Love it," Gwen answered.

At the table she blurted out, "I didn't understand it at all. Hardly a minute."

Jack looked surprised. "Of course you did. Just think about it."

"No," Gwen said firmly. "I didn't. There were these three guys and this girl, but I have no idea how they related to each other. Really."

Jack smiled. "You're just blocking, because you're used to words all the time. You'll see. The next one you'll understand."

Gwen felt something inside of her curl. There were going to be *more*? But she persisted. Something driving her on. "What did the little guy want the girl to do?"

Jack took her hand and kissed it. "It doesn't matter. But . . . he was her father and he wanted her to marry the rich man."

He was right. It didn't matter. What mattered were his lips against her hand and the way his eyes looked into hers, never wavering, never leaving hers.

When the waitress came to the table, Jack asked, "What kind of pizza?"

"Anything without anchovies."

They ate the pizza, helping each other curl the long strings of cheese into their mouths, filling glasses from the soda bottles on the table: Jack reached over and wiped a smear of cheese off Gwen's nose. And part of all of that time, they looked at each other, saying nothing, letting tides of intense feeling rise up over them and recede.

In the car, Jack moved out of the lot quickly and drove to the beach. It was not any of the spots kids frequented. He stopped the car on a rise overlooking the water. There were no streetlights, no moon. They could hear the ocean, smell it, and feel the fog that rolled in from it, but they could barely see it. Just a dark outline of power and the continuing sound of the roll that would go on forever.

He reached over and took Gwen in his arms and kissed her. Her arms went up around his neck, and his arms tightened around her. Then she pulled away.

"No," she said. "I mean . . . I . . . just no."

Jack let go immediately. "OK. OK. Don't get upset. It's OK."

Gwen looked out into the blackness, looking for some kind of landmark to tell her where she was. "I just . . ."

Jack turned her face to his. "You don't have to say anything. I heard you."

He touched her lips lightly with his and reached over and turned on the radio. A Crystal Gayle record came on and Jack held Gwen's hand as they listened silently.

He'll never ask me out again, Gwen thought. *Probably.*

Then Jack asked, "What do you want to do tomorrow night? How about a movie in English?" He laughed as he squeezed her hand.

Gwen cried out silently. "I can't tomorrow night, Jack."

He turned to face her. "You don't take violin lessons on Saturday nights too?"

Gwen giggled softly. "I don't know how to say this but . . .

48

there's this boy. He lives next door, just like the TV sitcoms, and I have a date with him tomorrow night."

Jack laughed. "Well, just tell him you can't see him. It's easy."

"No, it isn't easy. We've been sort of going together for years. He was mad because I was seeing you tonight."

"Gwen, are you going steady with this guy?"

Gwen twisted in the seat and listened to the sound of the ocean. It usually made her so happy, so relaxed, but tonight it pounded in her ears uncomfortably. "I guess I have been . . . until I met you . . . but now . . ."

"Now what?"

"I want to be with you."

"And I want to be with you. So you've just got to tell this guy you're going to be dating me."

"Jack, I can't just cut him out of everything. Are you saying you want to see me every weekend?"

Jack laughed and kissed Gwen's cheek. "Darling, Gwennie. I'm not saying yes every weekend and I'm not saying no. I'm not being difficult or evasive or mean. I just don't live like that . . . with every weekend known three weekends before. I just know, I just know I want to see you . . . a lot."

Gwen felt a tear wandering down her face. A tear of confusion. A tear of fear. A tear of guilt. "I'll talk to Michael."

She wasn't going to stop seeing Michael. How could she? He was her friend. He was her growing-up companion. Suddenly she was cold and the ocean fog was not welcome, well-known. It was a cover of chill and grayness that she tried to shrug off. Jack, seeing her slight shiver, started the car.

"You're cold. I'll take you home." At the same time, he put on the heater and Gwen leaned toward the first blast of warmth that filled the car.

In front of her house, Jack reached for her and held her in his arms. "You're special, Gwen. You're my special girl."

49

Gwen didn't know what he meant by that and didn't ask. It was enough just to snuggle in his arms and listen to his even breathing. When he kissed her, she answered him with all the feeling welling in her.

Finally he leaned away from her, "I'll call you," he said.

Gwen didn't wait for him to get out. She ran out of the car and at her door she turned and waved to him. He leaned to his left and looked out of the window she had closed. He waved back.

Inside her house she wondered when "I'll call you," would be.

A little later, lying in bed, she thought about why she had stopped Jack when he was kissing her. When Michael kissed her, she only responded with tenderness and warmth. When Jack kissed her, it had elicited feelings in Gwen she had never had before.

So that's what it's all about, Gwen thought. The things some of her friends had discussed, all the exciting, explicit books she had read made sense now.

She fell asleep smiling, thinking of the sweetness and excitement and uniqueness of Jack O'Neal.

CHAPTER 7

Before Gwen was fully awake the next morning, she felt a rock in her stomach and a free-floating anxiety she couldn't locate. Then it spilled over her. Tonight she had to tell Michael something . . . what?

She dressed that night as carefully as she had for Jack, thinking if she looked too casual Michael would think she didn't care enough about him to bother looking too good. And if she dressed up too much, he might think just the opposite.

When Michael rang the bell at eight, she was ready, pulse racing, mouth dry, palms sweaty. Her stomach turned over when she looked at him, hair slicked down, still wet from a shower, freshly shaven, smelling of a woodsy after-shave lotion. He was so familiar, so dear.

He kissed her lightly on the cheek. "What do you want to do? Movie . . . The Joint . . . drive around?"

Gwen touched Michael's arm lightly. "Michael, could we just go somewhere and talk . . . somewhere quiet."

A light came to Michael's eyes.

"No," Gwen said quickly. "That's *not* what I mean. I mean talk . . . really."

Michael shrugged. "No one is home at my house. That OK? The light was still in his eyes.

Gwen summed up the situation and decided it would be easier to talk alone at Michael's.

"OK. Your house."

As they walked to his front door Gwen said quickly, "Let's just sit in the living room."

On the couch, Michael reached for Gwen and she moved away. "Michael, listen, there's something I have to say."

"OK. Say."

Gwen got up and moved across the room to the windows and stared out. Then she turned back to Michael. "Don't you think we're too young to date just each other? Wouldn't you like to take out other girls besides me?"

"No." Michael answered immediately and firmly.

"Well, you know, what about that Patty Thomas. I've seen you looking at her with interest. You *know* you'd like to take her out."

Michael answered, "What's with you, Gwen? What's this sudden concern with my social life?"

Gwen went back to the couch and sat down, staring at her hands. "I guess I'd like to feel I could date another guy . . . if I wanted to."

"You mean Jack O'Neal, don't you? It isn't *other* guys you want to date . . . it's *one* guy. Right?"

Gwen felt tears welling in her eyes. "Well, yes. I mean I would like to . . . but I want to see you too. I'm not saying I don't want to see you."

"Thanks a bunch, Gwen. You're really thoughtful," Michael said with anger.

Gwen reached for Michael's hand and now tears were slowly trickling down her cheeks. "Michael, I care about you. I do, but I just have to . . . have to see Jack too. Try to understand. Please."

Michael reached in his pocket, took out a crumpled tissue, and handed it to Gwen. "Don't cry. Just don't cry!"

He looked at Gwen's hand in his and then at her face, which was filled with a plea, a hope, and running mascara.

"What's so special about O'Neal? All this time we've just dated each other. Now . . . suddenly . . . this creep comes along and . . . what's so different about him?"

"I don't know, Mike. He probably isn't as nice as you are, but I . . . I don't know." Gwen's voice rose up to a frantic pitch and she twisted Michael's hand.

Michael watched the tears rolling down Gwen's cheeks, quickly now. "OK. I've always been a sucker for your tears. I don't think it's going to work, but we'll try. We'll see other people." He jumped up. "I don't want to talk about this any more. I'll have to think about it later. Come on, we'll go to The Joint for a Coke or a burger."

It was like Michael. He didn't deal with things at the moment they happened. He reacted and then thought about it later when he could sort out what he was feeling. He seemed unable to know what he really wanted to do about anything immediately but needed time to examine and analyze a given situation.

They stayed at The Joint for an hour and then went home much earlier than usual. At Gwen's door Michael said, "I don't want to come in tonight. I'll see you tomorrow." He kissed her cheek and ran down the path from the door.

— ♥ —

Monday afternoon was brilliantly sunny with small puffy clouds that sailed across the sky. When Gwen came out of school, the sweet-smelling air was filled with the delicate odor of new leaves. Her breath caught in her throat when she saw Jack leaning against the wall that bordered one side of the high school. The sun was hitting his hair in a way that made him look golden and almost ablaze with light.

He walked toward Gwen as she came toward him. "I have a picnic in the car. We'll go to the beach? OK?"

Gwen hesitated for a moment. She had told Manda she might come over. But then Gwen smiled and said, "Sure. Great."

They drove to a part of the beach that rarely had much

traffic and in April was totally deserted. Jack pulled a blanket and a picnic basket out of the car and they trudged through the sand to a spot as close to where the ocean rushed in as they could. The sun sparkled off the waves, which tossed silver spray into the air.

Jack spread out the blanket and unpacked the basket as Gwen watched every movement he made, unable to take her eyes away from him to help.

Jack looked up and motioned to the food. "What do you want? We have three kinds of cheese, French bread, fruit."

Gwen pointed to one of the cheeses and Jack sliced off a hunk and put it on a piece of crusty bread. He handed it to her.

Jack hauled a large bottle of Coke out of the basket. "Coke?" He smiled.

Gwen nodded yes, thinking that he was considerate as well as bewitching. Considerate and yet she often felt odd with him. Then she was flooded with anger at herself.

Gwen hugged her knees to her chest and gazed at the tumultuous ocean. "You make me feel so . . . so off base at times. As if you're laughing at me."

Jack was silent. Then he answered softly. "I'm not laughing, Gwen. Never have been."

Gwen turned to him and cried out. "What do you want with me? I mean, what attracts you to me? We're so different. At least I think we are. One moment you make me feel as if I'm floating away somewhere and the next I feel leaden."

Jack opened the bottle and carefully poured a glass of soda. "You're the first person I've ever known who I felt knew where she was going and how to get there."

"And you like that?"

"Yes, I like it."

Gwen poured white, pearly sand from one hand to another. *Now is the time*, she thought. "I'm going to be a lawyer."

"See," Jack said, "that's what I mean. Most kids would say, 'I think I'm going to be a lawyer' or 'Maybe I'll be a lawyer,' but you know. You say 'I'm going to be a lawyer.' It's a good thing to be too. Lawyers can make a lot of money."

Gwen said vigorously, "No! Not that kind. I want to help poor people who get into trouble and don't know were to get advice and can't afford to pay for it."

Jack looked puzzled. "I've never thought about that. I mean, I don't know people like that."

Gwen looked directly at him, at the amber eyes with the yellow flecks. "Jack, the world is full of people who are poor and hungry and alone. People who are the wrong color or the wrong religion or the wrong sex or speak the wrong language in the wrong place."

Jack stared at Gwen briefly. Then he grinned his beautiful grin and pushed her down on the blanket. He looked into her eyes and said, "I see a white, lovely cloud reflected in your eyes. It's drifting slowly by, drifting, drifting, now, now it's gone."

He bent his head and kissed her slowly. The poor, the hungry fled from her mind and all she was aware of was the sun on her legs and the sand shifting beneath the blanket and Jack's kiss. Her arms moved up and around his neck and his hands cradled her face.

It would be so easy . . . Gwen sat up and reached for the Coke. Her hands were unsteady as she opened it and poured a glass.

He sat up and drank some of the soda. They were silent and then he asked, "Did you talk to the guy? The boy next door."

Michael. Michael. "Yes. I told him I wanted to date other people."

"What did he say?"

"He said he didn't think it would work for him, but he'd try it."

Jack looked down at his glass. "He loves you."

Gwen shrugged. "I guess, but I don't love him."

Jack grinned again, and reached out and smoothed Gwen's wind-blown hair back from her face. "Good."

Gwen smiled back, a radiant, happy smile. "What do you want to do when you're older?"

Jack thought. "Do? Well . . . I want to see everything there is to see in this world. I want to eat oranges in Spain and chestnuts in Paris and artichokes in Rome."

Gwen felt uncomfortable. Frightened. Yet she was intrigued by his answer and she pressed on. "And then? After you've eaten the oranges and the chestnuts and the artichokes. Then?"

Jack laughed and kissed her nose. "Then I'll go to the Easter Islands and Tahiti and the South Pole."

Before she could lose herself in the picture of him on trains and planes, always leaving for somewhere she wasn't, he said, "Saturday night. How about Greek food Saturday night? There's this cheap place in Seaview where they do Greek dances and sing and we should go."

"Sounds wonderful."

Jack pushed her back again and kissed her once more. Just once. Sweetly, tenderly, slowly. Then he stood. "It's five o'clock. I have to pick up my father in New York. We're going to a baseball game."

They packed up the basket and walked back to the car, holding hands tightly, sand crunching between entwined fingers.

He was at school on Tuesday afternoon too. When Gwen saw him, she felt a momentary stab of anxiety and she shifted her violin from one hand to another. But then he was at her side, taking the violin from her and saying, "I know! You have a lesson. I just thought I'd drive you there."

Her heart lifted and swelled like a slow-rising ocean wave. She linked her arm through his and smiled into his eyes.

When they were in his car, he turned on the ignition, and asked, "Which way?"

She gave him instructions and was surprised when he stopped in an empty lot. He turned to her and said, "I want to hear you play."

"Now?" Gwen asked, astounded.

"Now."

"I can't play in the car. That's impossible."

Jack reached over Gwen and opened the door. "We'll get out and you can play here. No one is around."

Gwen got out and opened the violin case. She adjusted the strings, set the violin under her chin, and played a part of a Beethoven violin concerto. She closed her eyes so that he wouldn't distract her and played with all her heart, wanting to be the best she could be at that moment. When she stopped and lowered the instrument, he was gazing at her with rapt admiration.

"You're good. Really good."

Gwen laughed. "No. Not really good. I have the feeling but not the technique. A Heifitz, an Isaac Stern, has both. I'll never be more than so-so, but I love it anyway."

Jack took the violin and put it back in the case. In the car, he took her into his arms and just held her.

They were silent.

Then he started the car again. "What kind of Greek food do you like?"

Gwen had to take a deep breath to carry herself from the intimacy of the moment before to the casualness of the present. She felt buffeted, unbalanced, but she tried to respond to him, wanting only to go back to his arms.

— ♥ —

When the phone rang in Gwen's room at nine that night, she knew who it was.

"I just wanted to tell you, you're beautiful," he said.

Gwen almost said "not really," but she caught herself thinking, *go with it*. "Thanks," she whispered, making it a caress.

"Good night," Jack said and she knew she was grinning.

"Good night, Jack O'Neal."

Beautiful. She went into the bathroom where the light was bright and looked in the mirror. Large brown eyes, seeming larger than ever. Curly brown hair. A mouth that was shaped by a boy's kisses, and a long straight nose. Beautiful?

Gwen turned when she heard a sound, and her mother was standing, watching her.

"Am I beautiful?" she asked.

Celia Warren looked at her daughter carefully. "I think so, but I'm naturally prejudiced."

Gwen kissed her mother lightly and went into her room, shutting the door behind her. Mrs. Warren stood for a moment and stared at the shut door.

CHAPTER 8

The pattern was set. Jack was there outside school every afternoon. Every night some time between nine and eleven, he called. They spoke briefly, but his voice echoed in her dreams for the rest of the night.

On Saturday night, they went to the Greek restaurant Jack had mentioned. Gwen ate moussaka and pastry dripping with honey and danced with strangers in the restaurant. Most of them were Greek and they danced with abandon and love and joy, as Jack did.

Gwen did not doubt it any longer nor was she afraid to say the words to herself. *I'm in love*. She waited for him to say it to her but he didn't.

Her days began only when she saw Jack waiting for her after school and they ended when she hung up the phone after his call at night. In between was time that was filled with thoughts of him, memories of him, and dreams of their future. She saw Michael one more evening after their talk and he had been right; it didn't work. She was uptight all night and Michael was angry, and so without discussing it they stopped dating altogether. They would wave when they saw each other. They hung over the bushes that separated their homes and talked, but always about superficial things. And there was always a question in Michael's eyes that Gwen couldn't answer.

It was Manda who reacted the most vocally to Gwen's absorption with Jack. "Do you think we could get together and talk some time this year?" Manda asked one day as they were changing classes. There was laughter in her voice but not in her eyes.

"Oh, Manda. Sure. I'm sorry. I've just been . . . well, you know."

"I know, but still . . . how about after school today?"

Gwen felt the blood rush to her face and for the first time in all the years since Manda had knocked her down the stairs, Gwen didn't know what to say to her.

"I can't. I mean Jack is always waiting for me. So . . ."

Let's grab a table for two in the cafeteria at lunch," Manda went on. "We can talk then."

"Sure. That's fine. Whoever gets there first gets the table."

Gwen was nervous for the rest of the morning for Manda was obviously disturbed by Gwen's unavailability. In the two and a half weeks since she had met Jack, she had seen very little of Manda. *So what? I'm not her mother. She has other friends.*

At lunch Manda picked at the salad on her tray and finally said, "Friends aren't something you dump because you have a boyfriend, Gwen."

"I haven't dumped you, Manda. I've just been . . ."

"Interested in one thing only," Manda said. Then she softened. "I know how you must be feeling. I mean, I've been in love. It's obsessive sometimes, but you have to try to keep your life going. You can't just focus on the guy."

"I don't seem to have room in my head for anything else but Jack," Gwen said.

"Look," Manda said, "Chuck and I are going to an Emmetts for President rally Saturday night. Why don't you and Jack come along?"

Gwen thought for a moment. "I don't even know if I'd vote for Emmetts if he got the nomination and I could vote. I'm not sure I like him."

"Me too. That's why I want to go hear what he'll say. Come on. It's over in Mineola. It could be fun."

"I don't know but I'll ask Jack. I've never heard him talk politics at all. He's not the political type, I don't think."

That afternoon she took Jack to her favorite place. It was the tallest dune on the beach and sitting at the top made you feel as if you were on the top deck of a ship, looking down on the ocean. The water was peaceful, with little, lazy waves that tapped quietly at the shore, hardly making a sound.

"Manda asked if we'd like to go to an Emmetts for President rally with her and Chuck Saturday night. Want to?"

Jack turned and looked at Gwen. "I don't know anything much about Emmetts."

"That's why they're going."

"It doesn't really matter much to me who gets elected president. It won't make any difference to me personally."

Gwen gazed out at the water. "But it *does* make a difference. If one guy is an environmentalist and one isn't, that's a big difference. Or if one is anti-bomb and the other isn't, that makes a difference."

Jack was silent and then. "To the world in general. But not to me. I mean, it doesn't affect my life today or tomorrow. So why bother?"

"I'm glad everyone doesn't feel like that," Gwen said quietly.

Jack turned and pulled Gwen into his arms. He kissed her. "Sweet, serious Gwen."

Then he kissed her again. She tried to hold on to Saturday night but she couldn't.

"I guess that means you don't want to go," she said when he let her go.

"There's this little coffeehouse in Greenwich Village I thought you'd like," Jack said. "I wanted to drive into New York and take you there. It's small and people just read poetry they've written or parts of books, whatever. It's highbrow like you." Jack grinned and pushed Gwen back onto the sand.

She looked into his amber eyes and asked warily. "Is that what you think? That I'm highbrow?"

"Sort of. I'm a playboy, you're not . . . a play*girl*, that is. You're more solid, more grounded."

Gwen looked away. "I'm not sure that's a compliment."

Jack turned her face back to his. "I mean it to be."

When she got home, she could hear her mother on the phone in the kitchen. Gwen ran up the stairs to her room and called Manda. *Get it over with*, she thought.

When Manda answered, Gwen said quickly, "Jack made other plans for Saturday night. So I can't go with you."

"Where are you going?"

"Oh, some coffeehouse in Greenwich Village where they read poetry and stuff."

"Sounds interesting," Manda said, but her voice was tight. "Do you *want* to go there?"

Gwen felt all the muscles in the hand and arm holding the phone contract. "Look, Manda. I'm not a wimp. I don't care where we go. I just want to be with Jack. OK?"

"OK. OK. Sorry. I'll see you tomorrow."

As Gwen hung up, her mother called loudly, "Gwen. That you?"

"Yes, Mom."

"Come down. I want to talk to you. *Now*."

She's upset. Now what? Gwen thought as she walked into the kitchen.

Her mother was sitting at the kitchen table reading a

novel, a cigarette dangling from her lips. Gwen reached for the cigarette and her mother grabbed Gwen's hand. "Don't."

Celia Warren jabbed the cigarette out vigorously in a shell-shapped ash tray. Gwen could almost hear her take a breath. "Gwen, you've been seeing Jack for over two weeks now . . . every day, every afternoon. What about your work? What's happening there?"

"I'm doing it, Mom. Don't worry." She thought fleetingly of a history exam she'd gotten back that day with a lower grade than she'd ever had in that class. She pushed the thought away and concentrated on small, silent waves weaving to the shore.

"If you're doing it, you're doing it late at night," Her mother said. "You're the only healthy, 16-year-old, middle class, overprivileged girl I know who has blue circles under her eyes."

Gwen looked into her mother's eyes. Her mother looked back. Their eyes held, neither looking away. The battleground was set.

"And Manda?" Mrs. Warren asked. "I haven't seen her since you met Jack. Where is she?"

Gwen kept her eyes riveted on her mother's. "She's busy too. I see her at school."

Gwen watched a nerve at the corner of her mother's mouth twitch once, twice. "And Michael. What's happened to him?"

Gwen closed her eyes for a moment. "He knows about Jack . . . and he doesn't want to see me while I'm dating Jack. I mean, he wants to see me, but not date. You know."

Celia Warren shook her head. "So you're up half the night, *maybe* doing your homework; you don't see Manda; and you don't see Michael."

Gwen got up suddenly. "Don't, Ma. Don't! I'm not a baby. Let me alone."

Gwen walked toward the kitchen door, trying to keep her head high and her shoulders back.

"Gwen," her mother called after her, "Gwen. *Think*."

— ♥ —

Saturday night was, well, different. The coffeehouse was trying hard to look like a movie version of a 1960 Village coffeehouse. There were mostly kids in their teens and early 20s there, trying to look like Village 1980s kids. Some of the poetry they read was good, very good; some was awful. Gwen tried to concentrate on what they were reading, but her mind drifted away and she wondered what Emmetts was saying. After four cups of strong coffee, she said to Jack, "If I have one more coffee, I won't sleep until I'm 26."

When they got back to Seaview, they parked in the place they had first gone to. There was a full moon. It drenched the water with silver and Gwen could barely look at the beach, it was so mystical and overwhelmingly beautiful.

Jack kissed her once and then again before she pushed him away.

"I want to go home, Jack."

"OK. No sweat." He reached over and pushed the hair off Gwen's forehead.

That was it . . . "no sweat."

Gwen stared out at the dazzling water, watching the radiant waves surging into the shore.

Gwen was suddenly tired. *I hardly understand him at all*, she was thinking. He could be from another planet. But when he left her at her door, kissing her thoroughly and whispering, "Gwen, Gwen," she knew she understood enough.

CHAPTER 9

When Gwen got out of school Monday afternoon and the sun touched her face with a combination of surface warmth and underlying coolness, she suddenly realized it was the end of April. Summer was near and she imagined what it would be like to have whole days to spend with Jack, long lovely days to laugh and love and enjoy.

She walked to the place where Jack was usually leaning against a brick wall and saw that he wasn't there. She looked around the school grounds, her eyes quickly passing over the crowds of kids leaving school. He wasn't there. She leaned against the wall, waiting for him, thinking he was caught in traffic or his car had broken down or run out of gas. After 15 minutes, she slumped down onto the cool ground, leaning back against the wall. Watching the street he would be coming from, she felt a wonderful anticipation, knowing the flood of feeling that would overtake her when she saw him.

When she looked at her watch, she was startled to realize 45 minutes had gone by since she had first come out of school. A small cold seed of anxiety planted itself somewhere inside her. She couldn't have said where. Stomach? Brain? Heart?

At four-thirty she stood up, thoughts whipping through her mind. He was hurt. He was dead. He didn't care. She got on a bus, and as soon as she got home ran upstairs to her room. She quickly dialed his number and let it ring 23 times.

Her fingers were cold and clumsy as she hung up the phone.

Suddenly she saw the accident. The car going a little too fast and running off the road, hitting a tree. She watched it turn over, the wheels spinning madly. *He's hurt. He's in the hospital. I know it.*

There was only one hospital in the area and she grabbed the phone book and looked up the number.

When the operator said, "Middle County Hospital," Gwen asked, "Do you have a patient named Jack O'Neal there?"

"I'll connect you with Admissions."

Gwen felt a surge of embarrassment as she waited for the clerk. *What was she doing? This was crazy.*

"Can I help you?"

"Yes. Do you have a patient named Jack O'Neal?"

"I'll check. One minute, please."

Gwen waited, her palms sweating so much that the phone was slipping her grasp.

"I've checked our records. There is no one by that name here."

"Thank you," Gwen breathed.

He wasn't hurt. He was all right. Relief made her slip down to the floor and lean against the bed. She reached up for the phone and dialed Jack's number again, listening to the repeated, unanswered rings.

Idiot, she thought. *He's probably trying to get you and you're keeping the phone busy checking hospitals.*

She got up, stretched out on the bed, and waited for his call. She watched the room get darker as twilight came and then evening.

"Gwen? Are you home?" her mother shouted from downstairs.

"Yes, I'm here."

"Well, dinner is ready. Come down."

At the table her mother looked at her with annoyance. "I

thought you hadn't gotten home yet. You could have helped with dinner, you know. Or were you studying?" Celia Warren's tone went from angry to hopeful.

"Umm. No, I was just sort of resting."

Gwen picked at her dinner, barely eating and not speaking at all. All she was doing was listening for her phone to ring.

"Are you OK, Gwen?" her father asked. "You look strange."

Gwen forced herself to smile. "I'm fine, Dad. Just a little preoccupied."

"I wonder with what," her mother said sarcastically.

Gwen pushed her plate away from her. "I'm not hungry. I'll go up and do some homework. Call if you want help cleaning up."

Upstairs Gwen dialed Jack's number again and listened to it ring. She let it ring endlessly, knowing that when she hung up she wouldn't be able to stand the silence. She lay on her bed almost motionless untill 11 o'clock when she dialed his number once more. But when his mother answered, she couldn't bring herself to ask for Jack. It was 11 at night; she had never met the woman; what would she think of a girl who would call her son that late? Gwen slowly, carefully, hung up the receiver, hoping it didn't make a click.

She slept that night from exhaustion and woke to an anxiety that had grown from a seed to a green shoot. She floated through the day hardly aware of anything she saw or heard, and ran out at three *knowing* Jack would be there. Manda was standing against the wall where Jack usually was, but wasn't today.

"I'm not horning in but I missed you at lunch. I wanted you to come to dinner tomorrow night," Manda said, her dark eyes moving over Gwen's face thoughtfully.

"Tomorrow? I don't know. 'I'm . . . I'm . . .'" The tears started falling, unexpected, uncontrollably.

"Gwen. What's wrong?" Manda reached into her bag for a Kleenex and stuffed it into Gwen's hand.

Between gulps and sobs and snatched breaths, Gwen said, "It's Jack. He just disappeared. He hasn't met me. He doesn't call. No one answers the phone . . . except his mother and I couldn't . . . I couldn't . . ."

Manda grabbed Gwen and started pushing her to the parking area. "I have my mother's car. I have to pick up some cleaning for her in town. Come on."

In the car, Manda asked, "Did you have a fight? Did something happen?"

"Nothing. Nothing. He just . . . he's just *gone*."

"Geez, Gwen, it's only a day. Relax. He'll call tonight."

Gwen looked at Manda and snuffled loudly. "Do you mean it? Do you really mean it?"

Manda ran her hands through her hair and said, "I don't know. It *is* funny; after the big rush, the nothingness. But some guys are like that. Easy come, easy go. Big deal and then goodbye, Charlie."

Gwen had stopped crying and sat silently shredding the wet tissue in her hand. "I feel as if I died. I don't even know me."

"Look, Gwen, call again, and if his mother answers, leave a message. You're not the kind of girl a guy has to keep from his parents, for heaven's sake. Leave your name. Tell his mother to have Jack call you. You can't just sit like a dummy and cry."

As soon as she got home, Gwen called Jack's house. When his mother answered, Gwen asked, "Is Jack there?"

Mrs. O'Neal's voice was soft, nice. "No. He's not here right now."

Gwen felt herself relax slightly. "When he gets in, will you ask him to call Gwen, please?"

"Sure, Gwen. Does he have your number?"

"Yes. Yes, he does. Thanks."

Her name had meant nothing to Mrs. O'Neal. Jack had never mentioned her at home. But boys were different, Gwen decided. They didn't necessarily share things like that with their parents. A girl's parents saw the guys calling for their daughter. They had to know more.

Gwen felt better. Jack would call tonight as soon as he got her message . . . but he didn't. The night was a repetition of the one before. The silent phone and Gwen stretched out on the bed waiting . . . waiting.

In the morning, Gwen knew what she had to do. At breakfast she said to her mother, "May I take the car to school? I have some things to do after school, errands and stuff."

Celia Warren pushed her scrambled eggs around on her plate. Then she looked at Gwen, her eyes filled with concern. "Take it. Just be careful. Gwen . . . listen . . . has something . . .?

Gwen jumped up from the table. "I can't talk now, Mom. I have to go. See you later."

At lunch Manda ran into the cafeteria and over to Gwen. "Did he call?"

Gwen shook her head no.

Manda sank down into a chair. "I would have called you last night, but I knew you'd have a fit when the phone rang and it wasn't Jack."

"I have my mother's car. I'm going to drive over to Westside this afternoon and wait for him to come out of school. I can't stand this nothingness."

Manda took a bite of her sandwich and said with a full mouth, "You'll have to cut your last two classes to get there before he gets out."

"I'd cut my throat to do it," Gwen said, trying to be funny but not able to get a smile up to her eyes.

"Want me to go with you?" Manda asked.

Gwen did smile now. "Thanks, Manda, but I'd rather go alone."

When Jack got out of school at two-fifteen, Gwen was standing at the side of the front entrance, watching the building empty. Her eyes raked over the kids streaming down the front stairs until she saw him. He was laughing and had on the scarf he had worn the first day he had appeared at her school. Gwen started toward him before she realized he was with two other boys, one on each side of him. They were all laughing and one of them playfully punched Jack on the arm. Jack feinted and pretended to punch him back while the third boy just watched, yelling something at Jack.

Gwen couldn't—no way could she go over to Jack when he was with his friends. It was too humiliating. What could she say in front on them? Where have you been? Why didn't you call? What's happened? Don't you love me any more?

She turned away and ran back to the car, driving out of the parking area too fast and not caring.

More than anything she wanted to skip dinner that night. How would she eat or speak? But she knew her parents would never accept her just not appearing at the table. So she sat with them, unaware of the chicken and potatoes and green peas on her plate, feeling that if she let one muscle relax she would fall into small pieces. All she saw was Jack laughing with his friends, not even thinking of the girl who was spending most of her waking hours waiting for him to remember her. He had looked as if she had never existed to him, as if she were a dream in her own mind.

"Gwen, I'm talking to you," her father's voice broke into her thoughts.

"I'm sorry. I didn't hear you."

"I said you look awful. Pale, nervous, not with it. What's going on?"

Celia Warren looked at Gwen anxiously. "Ethan, not now. Let her eat her dinner."

Mr. Warren shook his head. "If she were eating her dinner or had eaten the one last night or the night before, I wouldn't be telling her she looks awful."

Gwen clasped her hands tightly in her lap and thought, *I don't want to cry, not in front of them. I don't want to cry.* She looked down and said simply, "I look awful because I feel awful. And I feel awful because Jack seems to have dumped me. If you can't or won't accept that is why I feel awful, I don't care."

Gwen's mother asked quietly, "What do you mean 'dumped you'? How dumped?"

"I haven't seen him or heard from him since last Saturday. I called and left a message at his house and he hasn't returned the call. That's dumped, isn't it?"

Then she started to talk quickly, almost incoherently. "But that's just impossible. I mean I know he'll call eventually. A boy doesn't see you every day and then just disappear. He'll call."

Ethan Warren threw his napkin on the table. "The creep. The dumb, little creep. A girl like you—a wonderful girl like you and he just walks away. You're better off without him. He's no good, obviously."

Gwen felt the tears sliding down her face and she let them. "I knew you'd say something like that. You don't understand at all."

Celia Warren stared out of the window, then she said, "That's happened to me once. A boy, maybe like Jack made me feel like Cleopatra, called, saw me, sent flowers, the whole bit, and then one day that was it. I never heard from him again. The worst part of it was I kept waiting to hear from him—for weeks."

Gwen stood up and ran from the room. "I can't talk any more."

The rest of the week went by as if she were gliding on the surface of the days, never making contact with anything solid. Mostly she thought about what she must have done wrong. Why had he just gone? It must have been her fault in some way. She remembered a line from an Emily Dickinson poem: "After great pain, a formal feeling comes." That was how she felt—formal—apart, stiff, and mechanical. It was only when she was alone in her room at night that she could let the pain and confusion express itself in tears and groans. She had decided not to call Jack again, though time after time she reached for the phone and then pulled her hand away as though she had been seared. Once she dialed the number and hung up before it even rang.

She went over and over what could have happened. Did he have another girl? Had she bored him? Been too predictable, too rigid?

Everyone tiptoed around her as if she were an invalid. Her mother made Gwen's favorite dishes, her father slipped her extra money, and Michael even rang the bell one night to see if she wanted an ice-cream cone. Only Manda approached Gwen with openness and honesty.

On Friday after school, Manda asked, "What are you doing over the weekend?"

Gwen looked at Manda, trying to understand what she was asking. "Doing?"

"*Doing,*" Manda said firmly. "Like how about coming to the movies with Chuck and me tomorrow night?"

"I'm sure that Chuck would be just delighted to have me come along on your date."

"Chuck is a good guy. He won't mind. You can't sit home and vegetate."

"Manda, thanks, but I can't go with you and Chuck. The thought of it makes me want to throw up."

Manda put her arm around Gwen's shoulders and gave a gentle squeeze. "I understand, really. Listen, my mother gave me a message for you."

Gwen raised her eyebrows. "You told you mother?"

"Sure. She's very understanding about love things. My

72

father dumped *her*, after all. I don't let her know I think he was mean because I love him anyway, but he was."

"So what was her message?" Gwen was curious about how an older woman faced this kind of thing.

"Mom says that Camus says that anything that doesn't kill you makes you stronger."

Gwen stopped walking and asked, *"That's* her message? *That's* supposed to make me feel better?"

Manda shrugged. "If you think about it, it *is* reassuring."

"You're crazy. How reassuring? You mean I should feel elated because Camus doesn't think I'm going to die, when I think I am."

Manda laughed softly. "Oh, you know my mother. She's deep."

Gwen smiled weakly. "Give your mother this message from me. Ask her if she and Camus can't come up with another way for me to get stronger."

CHAPTER 10

The next morning Gwen and her mother sat at the breakfast table in silence. Gwen moved Rice Krispies around in the bowl and Celia Warren stirred her coffee over and over.

Finally she asked, "What are you going to do over the weekend? Any plans?"

"No. I don't know, just . . ." Gwen looked at her mother and there was a desperate, pleading expression in her eyes. "I'd like to borrow your car and go to the beach. May I?"

"Are you going to look for Jack? You're not going to do that, are you, Gwen?"

Gwen shook her head. "No! No! Really! I just want to be by myself and sit on the beach. I'm not going where I met him. I have my own place . . . a private place. I want to go there. Please."

Mrs. Warren kept stirring her coffee. "I don't like you to drive when you're upset. It worries me, Gwen."

Gwen begged softly. "I won't be upset if I can just sit near the water. I'll be fine. I'll be careful. Ma, please."

Celia Warren sighed deeply. "All right. But please watch your driving. And, listen, if you have the car, you'll have to stop at Adrienne's and give her a jacket she left here during the week. She'll need it."

Gwen didn't want to see Adrienne, but if that was the price she had to pay for the car, she'd pay it.

As she drove to the beach, she counted the weeks since she had made the same drive and had seen Jack for the first time. Four weeks. One month. Twenty-eight days. The girl behind the wheel today seemed to bear no connection to the girl of four weeks before. The only thing that bound them together was their feeling about Adrienne. Gwen didn't even think she looked like the other girl. That one had clear eyes and a quick smile and a low laugh. This Gwen's eyes were clouded with anguish; her smile had disappeared; and her laughter had a high, forced quality to it, when it came at all.

Jack, she thought. *Oh, Jack. What happened? What did I do?*

She parked the car outside the sandy entrance to her beach and walked to the high dune and sat down. The beach was deserted, quiet, as it had been before . . . long before the first humans had discovered it and tried to make it their own . . . something they never could do really. It would always belong to itself, allowing people to borrow its warmth and strength and tides from time to time, but only lending them.

Slippery green seaweed covered the tideline, holding white and gray shells captive in its sticky ooze. The ocean rolled and heaved in and out, like the pain in Gwen, only Gwen's never rolled out. She watched the water and concentrated on one wave, a ribbon of white at the horizon that moved with quiet, uncontested force closer and closer to the shore. She watched it rise high, with green lights covering its underside. It gathered speed as it raced to dash itself on the shore. The tide pulled it out, out, and it merged with the sea to start its cycle all over again.

It would never end. It comforted Gwen in a way she could not understand. But she accepted the comfort, embraced it, and let it pull some of the hurt from her and toss it into the roaring water. She sat there for two hours, barely moving, letting the rhythm of the water become her mantra and letting Jack recede with the waves. When a family with two small children trudged onto the beach and started unpacking toys and food and a radio, Gwen got up and walked back to the car.

She drove to Adrienne's, parked the car, and took the jacket. Adrienne lived in a garden apartment in a small housing project filled with newlyweds and couples with small children. When Adrienne opened the door to Gwen's ring, she was munching on a peanut-butter sandwich. She was surprised to see her sister.

"Hi," she said, waving the sandwich. "What's up?"

Gwen held out the jacket. "You left this last week. Mom asked me to deliver it."

"Well, come in. Don't just stand in the hall. Davey is napping. Want a sandwich?" The words tumbled out.

"Sure, I'll have a sandwich. I haven't had any lunch."

As they walked through the living room into the kitchen, Gwen noted the playpen and carriage and assorted toys as well as unfolded laundry and unread newspapers that were strewn around the room. The kitchen matched the living room, with dishes waiting to be put into the dishwasher, groceries needing to be put away, and a basket of clothes that needed washing in a corner.

As Adrienne made the sandwich, she nodded in the direction of the mess. "I'm a little behind. As usual."

"It doesn't bother me," Gwen said. There was silence, both of the young women thinking of what to talk about to cover the awkwardness they were feeling.

Finally Adrienne said as she pushed a plate toward Gwen, "You look drawn and tired. What's wrong?"

"You mean Mother hasn't given you a blow-by-blow?"

Adrienne flushed slightly. "Well, yes, she did mention that Jack wasn't around or something like that."

"I thought she would." Gwen felt anger flood through her. "I seem to be everyone's favorite topic of conversation."

Adrienne ignored the bitterness. "Want to tell me?"

Gwen didn't, but she couldn't think of a way out that wasn't cruel. So she told Adrienne what had happened during the last week, ending with ". . . and I haven't seen or heard from him since."

Adrienne twisted a glass of milk around and around on the table. "Well, it must be interesting to have something unexpected happen in your life. Something unplanned, unscheduled. It doesn't sound all bad to me."

Gwen remembered the night Adrienne had watched her trying to decide what to wear on her first date with Jack. "You said something like that before. Are you sorry you got married?"

"No, not really. I love Joe. I love Davey. I just would like not to be so caught in a routine that seems unchanging. I'd like to feel like 20 instead of 40."

Gwen just stared. Adrienne smiled slightly. "I'm sorry. You're miserable and unhappy and I just babble about myself."

Gwen looked at Adrienne directly. "Did you have to get married? I mean were you pregnant?"

"No," Adrienne shouted. "Everyone thinks that. I got married because I wanted to. I got pregnant right away and Davey really was premature."

"So why did you get married so young?"

Adrienne shrugged. "I loved Joe. I was a lousy student. Not like you. I had no feelings of wanting to be a doctor or a lawyer or even work at all. So it all seemed like a fun thing to do—a good escape from school, from home. I'd have a good time, I thought. Then I got pregnant and I wanted the baby.

77

I still want him and Joe, just a little less of the time than I've got them."

Gwen finished the sandwich and wiped her mouth. "When Joe earns more money, you'll be able to go out more. It will be different."

Adrienne brushed her hair out of her eyes and looked at Gwen. "Look at us. We're talking. Really talking to each other. It doesn't happen often, does it?"

Gwen shook her head no.

"I know you don't like me much, Gwen. I just never really understood why."

Gwen felt a flush cover her face and she looked away from Adrienne, embarrassment making her speechless. *Adrienne knew.*

"Don't look so embarrased," Adrienne said. "There's no law that says sisters have to like each other. It would just be nice. What did I ever do, Gwen, that makes you pull away whenever I'm around or try to talk to you?"

Impulsively Gwen reached out and grabbed Adrienne's hand. "I don't know. Or I do. It's just that you always seemed to get all the attention, to be the one doing something for the first time."

Adrienne's eyes widened. "Really. I always thought *you* were the one getting all the attention. You were the smart one, the serious one, the one who was going to amount to something. I was just, well . . . Adrienne. Not much. Not special . . . just me."

The two sisters looked at each other and then they laughed. They didn't try to go any further than they had. Ground had been broken, but it had been frozen so long that it was stiff.

Gwen looked around the apartment. "You know, if you straightened up a little you might feel better. Come on, I'll help you."

Adrienne stood up and pulled her T-shirt over her stomach. "Not today. Davey will be up soon. Some other time."

The moment had passed, but as they retreated to their separate corners, the gulf between them seemed a little less awesome.

"I have to go," Gwen said.

Adrienne walked her to the door. "I think he'll call some time. I really do. You'll see.

Gwen knew she didn't mean it, but she leaned over and kissed her. "Give Davey a hug for me."

Driving home, Gwen tried to sort out her feelings. If *she* thought Adrienne were getting all the attention, and Adrienne thought *Gwen* were getting all the attention, who was the one *really* getting it? What was the reality, when she and Adrienne each had their own truth? And now what? Was she supposed to feel sorry for Adrienne? Was she supposed to like her, even love her? It was easier when things were crystal clear to Gwen—when she was sure she had been the neglected child and Adrienne the lucky center of love. Now she had to try to look at Adrienne and herself in different lights, and she really didn't want to. Especially now, when her whole being was filled with Jack, when there was no room in her head for sibling relationships and rivalries and futures. It didn't seem important any more. And yet she knew when she had exorcised Jack, Adrienne would once again be a major irritant in her life.

After dinner that night, she went to her room and lay on the bed in the dark. She tried to make her mind an empty, spongy grass mass—empty of pain, empty of love, empty of hope. She heard cars going down the street, an occasional burst of laughter from someone walking by, and the slapping of the shade against the window in her room. The sounds drifted in and out of her head until her mother knocked at the door.

"Michael is downstairs."

Gwen got up. "Michael? What does he want?"

"I didn't ask him, Gwen. He wants to talk to you."

Gwen turned on the light and blinked at the sudden brightness. She ran her fingers through her hair and walked down the stairs slowly.

Michael was in the living room, from which her parents had magically disappeared. He turned toward her as she walked into the room. How nice-looking he is, Gwen thought. Not golden, not bewitching, just nice.

"I thought you might like to go to a movie . . . or for a drive . . . or something," he said tentatively.

"Why? Why do you want to be with me? I haven't exactly been very nice to you lately."

"You're right, you haven't but honestly, Gwen, you've been looking so gross this week . . . so pale and . . . I just thought you might want some company."

"You mean it's your good deed for the day. How many more do you have to do before you get your Boy Scout medal or something?"

Michael flushed and then his mouth tightened. "Bug off, Gwen. Forget it."

As he moved toward the front door, Gwen ran after him. "I'm sorry. Please forgive me. I'm just weird these days. I don't deserve you even as a friend."

Michael looked at her. "That's all I was trying to be, Gwen. A friend. That's what we were before we were . . . whatever. Jack O'Neal might be able to do a lot of things, but I'm not going to let him louse up what once was a good friendship."

Gwen sank down on the bench that was next to the door. "Why are you so good and he's so . . . ?"

Michael looked down at her and shrugged. "I'm not so good. Don't canonize me. I just want to take you to the movies, not reshape your life."

Gwen laughed. "Thanks, Michael. But not tonight. Some other time. OK?"

"OK," Michael said and left the house.

Gwen sat on the bench for a long time, wondering why, when she fell in love for the first time, it couldn't have been with Michael.

CHAPTER 11

Gwen left school Monday afternoon with Manda. Willing herself not to, but unable to deny her need, Gwen looked to the spot against the wall where Jack used to wait for her. She knew he wouldn't be there, but she wanted just to look at the place where he once stood. The sunlight hit the wall, splaying shadows onto the ground.

The sunlight also hit Jack O'Neal, making his hair look like molten gold. He *was* leaning against the wall!

Gwen stopped walking and remained motionless. Manda put her hand on Gwen's arm and tried pulling her along. "Come on, Gwen. Keep moving. Don't stop."

Jack raised his hand, waved at her, and walked, in that loose liquid way of his, over to her. When he got to her side, he kissed her cheek, "Hey. You look beautiful."

Gwen felt Manda pulling on her arm again. "Don't, Manda, don't."

"Gwen," Manda said, pleading.

"Just let me alone. I have to talk to him."

Manda gave Jack a quick look and shook her head in despair. "Call me later."

Jack put his arm around Gwen's shoulders. "The car is in the parking lot."

"Where have you been?" Gwen asked. Her voice was tight and high and almost inaudible.

"What do you mean, 'where have I been'?"

"It's been a week," Gwen said. "I haven't seen you or

heard from you in a week!" She hated the accusatory tone in her voice; she wanted to seem laid back, uncaring, as he was uncaring.

"But I told you," Jack said. "I told you that I was going to be tied up last week. That I was putting a car together with some of the guys."

"No," Gwen yelled, not caring about anyone around her. "No, you didn't tell me anything. You just weren't here. You just didn't call and you didn't tell me."

Jack stepped back and she could see him going over words, times, places in his head. "I thought I did. I thought I had . . ."

"I don't understand you, Jack. I don't understand . . ." Gwen's voice broke.

Jack put his hand on her arm. "Please get in the car with me. Let me talk to you. Please, Gwen."

In the car, Gwen sat as far from him as she could. She huddled in the corner of the seat, her arms wrapped around herself, comforting herself. Jack looked out of the window in silence.

"Whatever you remember isn't so, Jack," Gwen began. "You just stopped coming to school, stopped calling me. I called and left a message with your mother. Did you get it?"

Jack turned to her. "Yes. She told me when I got in that night, but it was late and I didn't want to wake you."

"And the next day?" Gwen asked.

"The next day I woke up late, after you left for school and then . . . then I guess I just forgot."

Gwen huddled deeper into the seat. "Just forgot all about me?"

"No," Jack shouted. He reached for Gwen and pulled her into his arms. "I'd never hurt you, Gwen. Never deliberately. I really thought I had told you I wouldn't be around last week. I really did. I love you, Gwen. You've got to believe me. I wouldn't hurt you. Wouldn't."

Gwen saw the beginning of tears in his eyes. His arms held her tightly; the warmth of his body began to thaw the ice of the week alone, the week of fear and pain and isolation. And she clung to him. She believed him. She knew he hadn't meant to hurt her. He was just . . . just what she didn't know. But she didn't care. He was with her, holding her, and as she kissed him she let his kisses cloud her brain so totally that she didn't hear the question that was struggling to reach the surface of her mind.

When they separated, he stroked her cheek, wiping away her tears. "I'd die before I hurt you, Gwen. I don't know how this happened, but it never will again. I promise you. I love you."

She ran her hands over his bright, golden hair and smoothed it away from his forehead. "I believe you, Jack. I believe you. Don't be so upset. It's all right."

They walked on the beach for an hour, not speaking much but holding hands tightly. Gwen clung to his fingers—he had never told her he loved her before, she realized. They must have reached a new plateau in their relationship and he never would do anything like that again. She knew it.

They sat on top of a dune at the beach, and Gwen looked at the little clumps of plants that were like bonsai trees, small but fully formed entities. She wished she could be like them, so complete unto themselves. Jack pushed her back onto the sand and kissed her mouth and eyes and forehead. He murmured things she couldn't hear.

Then he jumped up and pulled her with him. "No more sadness. No more tears. We are going to have the best time we've ever had. Tell me what you want to do this weekend. Anything you want. Just name it. Paris? Rome? Disneyland?"

Gwen laughed and brushed the sand from her jeans. "Manda is having a party Saturday night. I want to go . . . with you. I want you to meet my friends."

"You've got it. We're going. I'll meet your friends and

your relatives and the whole *county* if you want."

Pure, silver waves of joy rolled through Gwen. He really *did* love her. He wanted to make her happy. She had come home. She was with Jack, where she wanted to be. The week of ice was gone and she was drowning in the sun that emanated from the boy she loved.

— ♥ —

She knew she was going to have to tell her parents that she would be seeing Jack again, and she dreaded thinking what their reaction would be. At dinner that night, she decided *not tonight*. She couldn't let her happiness be spoiled: happiness that was a combination of being with Jack again and relief that the anguish, the isolation, the aloneness she had been feeling were gone.

After dinner, she sat in her room and went over every word Jack had said. At the same time, she remembered Manda's "call me." What would Manda say?—as if she couldn't guess. As Gwen was looking at the phone and putting off reaching for it, she heard steps coming up the stairs and Manda's voice calling, "Hey, Gwen. You there?"

Manda walked into the room and sat down on the floor near Gwen. "You were going to call me."

"No. *You* said 'call me,' *I* didn't say I would."

Manda shruggd. "Semantics. So what happened?"

"I'll tell you, but don't give me a hard time. I won't listen to . . ."

Manda grinned. "Do I ever give you a hard time? Just tell me where he was all week."

"He was working on a car with some friends. He thought he had told me he would be tied up. He really thought he had."

"Sure, and I think I'm Princess Diana."

Gwen clenched her fists. She loved Manda, but sometimes, like then, she would have liked to punch her out.

85

"I told you, Manda, don't give me a hard time. I believe him, I love him, and I'm happy again, and we're coming to your party Saturday night, if you want us."

"OK," Manda said seriously. "So let's say it's true. He *thought* he told you he would be busy, that he couldn't see you or call you. Do you want that kind of guy for your boyfriend? I mean, is that OK with you?"

Gwen responded to Manda's concern, to her honest question, but it still made her feel resentful. Why did Manda have to cross-examine her, as if she were Lizzie Borden or something?

Gwen got up from her chair and stood over Manda. Looking down on her shining hair and intent dark eyes, she felt confused and sure, at the same time. Confused by why she was sure of what she felt.

"I want Jack, and if *that* is who he is, well, that's who he is. OK? Can we stop the questioning? I'm not on trial for any heinous crime, you know."

Manda stood up and watched the strange expression on Gwen's face. Manda had never seen her so defensive, so near real rage. She backed off, not wanting to jeopardize their friendship in anyway, not sure who this Gwen was.

"OK. I'll let you live your own life. It'll be hard, but I'll do it." Manda laughed and the awful moment was past. "And of course I want you to come Saturday night. Dumb question. I want to see this paragon in action."

Gwen laughed, too, relieved. "I've never seen him in action either. We've never been with other kids, always by ourselves. It's a big concession for Jack to come to your party."

"Big deal," Manda muttered. And then quickly, "Sorry. Sorry. Cross that off the record."

Manda opened the door leading out of the room. "I have to go. I have a report to write. Last-minute me."

As Manda walked out of the room, she whispered, "Have

you told your parents about Jack yet?"

Gwen closed her eyes and deliberately shuddered. "No. Won't *that* be gross?"

— ♥ —

Ten minutes before Gwen's last class ended the next day, she felt her hands get clammy. What if he weren't there today? What if he just didn't show . . . again?

When she left school, carrying her violin, she could hardly bear to look at what she thought of as "Jack's wall." What if?

But there he was, leaning against the wall, his eyes squinting against the sun. She ran over to him and he took the case from her hand. He kissed her cheek, grabbed her arm, and they ran to his car. In the car, he took her in his arms and kissed her. When she pulled away, she took his hand and kissed his palm and her fingers touched something cool around his wrist. A silver identification bracelet with the initials J. O'N. engraved on it circled the warm flesh.

"What's that?" she asked.

Jack looked down at the bracelet. "Pretty cool, isn't it? My mom gave it to me last week for my birthday. I always wanted something glitzy like that."

Gwen pulled back and looked at Jack, unable to believe it. "You had a birthday last week and I didn't even know. How could you not tell me?"

Jack laughed . . . that laugh. "I don't know when *your* birthday is. What's the big deal?"

"I know you don't. But if it were next week, I'd tell you. It isn't until September so it's different. But I feel as if something important happened and I didn't even know it was happening."

Jack pulled her close. "If it's *that* important to you, we'll celebrate Friday night. In fact we'll celebrate *your* birthday too."

Gwen felt cold. "Does that mean you don't expect to be seeing me in September? So let's celebrate now?"

Jack shook his head, his hair falling over his eyes as he did. "Gwen, I don't even know what you're talking about. It was a joke. I thought it would be fun."

As they drove to her violin lesson, Gwen thought, *What is with me?* He was back. Why was she looking for trouble? She was wary and realized she was trying to pin him down, to give herself some sense of security that didn't come with Jack's territory. The impossible dream.

She rested her head on Jack's shoulder and closed her eyes. "I'm sorry, Jack. Forget it. As Manda would say, 'cross that from the record.' "

He leaned his cheek against the top of her head. "Funny Gwen."

Adrienne and Joe and Davey came to dinner that night. Gwen looked around the table and thought it would be a good time to get it over once and for all. One agony and they'd *all* know.

During an unusual moment of silence, Gwen said loudly and firmly, "I'm seeing Jack again."

Everyone's eyes turned to her and, in a moment of clarity, Gwen saw each of their expressions separately. Her mother's concern; her father's anger; Joe's puzzlement; and Adrienne . . . what? She couldn't make out what Adrienne was thinking.

Gwen filled them in as briefly and calmly as she could. But she could hear the quiver in her voice and she was aware of one drop of perspiration slowly dripping down her side. Families were a pain. Why couldn't they just all let her live her own life? She was willing to take the hard knocks so why didn't they realize that?

Gwen's father said curtly, "Don't you have any self-respect? Don't you see the boy is conning you?"

"I don't think he is," Gwen answered and let her father

know by the silence that followed that one sentence that she wouldn't discuss it with him.

Celia Warren looked as if she were in actual pain. "Gwen, dear, a boy like that, you leave yourself open to such heartache."

"Well, it's my heart," Gwen said as firmly as she had answered her father.

"He seems very irresponsible, not dependable at all," Joe said, as if he couldn't imagine that a species of man like Jack existed.

"Maybe," Gwen said.

Now all she had to do was cope with Adrienne. Three down and one to go, unless Davey decided to speak his first full sentence at that moment.

Adrienne put her fork down and said to Joe, "So he's not the most responsible boy in the world. He sounds like he's fun and exciting."

Then she turned to her father and mother. "Why don't you leave Gwen alone? Let her do her own thing. She's not robbing banks or doing anything wrong. So what's all the criticism about? She's just doing what isn't bizarre at 16, falling in love. She's right on target."

Now I'm going to have to like her, Gwen thought. Never had she imagined that support would come from Adrienne. She sent her a look of gratitude and Adrienne smiled back at her. Their eyes locked. Wouldn't it be incredible if I had a sister after all?

Celia Warren stood up and started clearing the table. "I never compared dating Jack O'Neal to robbing banks, Adrienne. But I don't have to feel grateful that she's seeing him either."

"Second the motion," Ethan Warren said. "Watch it, Gwen. I don't like the guy, but if you want to see him, it's your skin. I just hate seeing you hurt."

"I'm not hurting," Gwen said. "I'm happy."

Adrienne started helping her mother stack dishes. "OK. Gwen has had her moment as the center of the Warren family attention; now let's talk about something crucial, like can you look after Davey while Joe and I go to the movies?"

The tenseness at the table was gone. Adrienne had saved Gwen from endless discussion and Gwen knew it. It was more than she could assimilate, however. As she got up to help Adrienne, her sister said, "Bring Jack over after school some time; I'd like to meet him."

Gwen shook her head in assent, feeling numb. Now her relief was complete. She had Jack again, she had told Manda, and she had told her parents. She felt the way she did when she ran into the ocean, exhilarated; the hard part, racing into the cold surf, was behind her. Now ahead was the big wave, roaring toward her, all excitement and encompassing, its clean, salty swirls surrounding her body. All she had to do was dive into it, become one with it, and feel the joy it brought.

The feeling of exhilaration was still there when she met Jack after school the next day. She was so wildly up that she immediately said, "Adrienne said we should come over some day after school. She wants to meet you."

Jack hesitated for a moment and then said, "Sure. Some day we'll do that."

"Today? Now?" Gwen asked. "I know she'll be home."

Jack grinned and took Gwen's hand, swinging it as they walked to the car. "Some day, not today. Today I'll just hold you in my arms. Or we'll build castles on the beach or go to a movie."

Gwen felt a small pinprick of disappointment. But an intuitive knowledge rising from a place of future understanding kept her silent except to say, "It's too late for the movies."

"That leaves hugging or castle building," Jack said. "Or a combination of both. We can either build castles and hug in

90

the car or on the beach. Different kinds of castles, of course, but both acceptable."

"What kind of castle would you build in the car?"

"Dream castles, naturally. Such as where you would most like to be this minute."

Gwen caught her breath. It was obvious where. "Here," Gwen said. "I wouldn't want to be anywhere but here with you."

Jack leaned over and kissed her cheek as they walked to the car. But it didn't satisfy Gwen. "Where would you like to be?"

She didn't want to hear his answer. She almost covered her ears with her hands and cried out, "Don't tell me." But she didn't.

"I'm thinking of Tahiti, maybe. Or Bali or Australia. Some place exotic and spellbinding.

She leaned her head on his shoulder when they got into the car. "You're spellbinding enough for me."

Jack kissed the top of her head. "You don't ask for much, Gwennie."

Gwen laughed a harsh laugh. "Too much, maybe."

He didn't call that night and Gwen lay in bed and looked at the ceiling, watching patterns drift across it, changing and moving, blending and separating. The ice returned.

But the next day, he was at the wall. "Sorry about last night. I went to the movies with Dad. I got in too late to call. But I thought about you, I really did, Gwen."

What did you think? she wondered.

CHAPTER 12

On Saturday Gwen felt a combination of anticipation and concern. Jack was unpredictable and how he would fit in with Manda's friends, her friends, was something she didn't know. She ached with wanting Jack to be liked, for the kids to accept him and make him part of the group. She realized, and then almost violently pushed it aside, that she had missed being with friends.

She wore a soft, pink dress that emphasized her shining hair and large eyes. It was warmer than usual for the beginning of May and the dampness in the air, coming from the sea, curled her hair wildly on her head. She brushed it, trying to make it all go in the direction she wanted, but it seemed to have a life of its own so that finally she just let it wind in soft, springing waves.

Jack looked wonderful. He had on khaki pants and a black shirt that made his caramel-colored hair look lighter. They drove to Manda's in silence.

Finally Gwen said, "Are you here? I mean, are you nervous about meeting all these new people or something?"

Jack threw his head back and laughed, making Gwen grab the wheel. "No, Gwen. I'm good at new people. You'll see. Are *you* nervous? Afraid I might disgrace you in some unmentionable way?"

"Of course I'm not nervous. I just want you to enjoy yourself and like my friends."

Jack squeezed Gwen's knee. "I'm already enjoying myself."

As soon as they arrived, Manda introduced Jack to everyone who was there. The names floated on the air, but Jack seemed able to grab them and make them part of his consciousness. He never faltered and called everyone by the right name immediately. The girls looked at him with undisguised interest, and Jack returned their looks with enough admiration to make them feel attractive, but not enough to upset Gwen.

The boys hung back. There was a new, good-looking guy on their turf, smiling at their girl friends. But within half an hour, Jack was the center of seven guys, and they were all talking about their cars, present and future. A few girls joined them, but basically the room had separated into boys and girls. Jack and the boys laughed a lot, shook their heads knowingly, and formed a tight circle.

Gwen watched, apart, an observer. "I'm good at new people." And he was.

Just when Gwen was beginning to feel that Jack had forgotten she was there, just as the other girls were beginning to get restless, and Manda's mouth was about to tighten, Jack broke away. He came over to Gwen and put his arm around her. "Want to dance?"

In his arms she let herself enjoy his closeness. "Are you happy?" she asked.

"Sure. It's a good party."

And it was. Jack was the magnet for all of them. Everyone drifted toward him, pulled by a strange force. The boys slapped him on the back and kept coming over to talk to him. The girls drifted close to him, asked him to dance, and laughed up at him encouragingly. There was an excitement in the room; something was happening—something charismatic. Manda's mother had come in ten minutes before and helped Manda bring out food and take away dirty glasses.

Only *she* seemed totally unaware of Jack. When Gwen and Manda and Vivian Perlstein were in the kitchen putting sandwiches on trays, Gwen said to Mrs. Perlstein, "Did you notice him?"

"Hard not to."

"Do you like him?" Gwen didn't know why she was asking Vivian instead of Manda, but somehow it was important.

Vivan pushed her blonde hair off her face. She smiled. "He's a charmer."

Then she wiped her hands on her jeans. "I'll disappear again. Can't have your friends think you have a hovering mother."

"Perish the thought," Manda said.

When Vivian left the kitchen, Gwen hugged herself. "I'm glad your mother liked him."

"How do you know she does?" Manda asked.

"Well, she said he was charming, didn't she?"

Manda looked thoughtful, far away. "She didn't say he was charming, she said, 'he's a charmer.'"

"It's the same thing, isn't it?" Gwen asked with annoyance.

Manda shrugged. "I don't know. Ask *her*, not me."

Gwen persisted. "What about you? Do you like him?"

"Sure. He seems . . . real nice. Fun, good-looking." Manda smiled, but it wasn't Manda's smile. It was bright and painted on.

Gwen left the party glowing. She clung to Jack's arm as they ran down the walk from Manda's house. She jumped into the car and waited for Jack to get in on his side. Then she threw her arms around his neck and kissed him. "You were wonderful. Everyone loved you."

Jack started the car and without asking drove to their parking place on the beach. "I need to have you to myself for a while."

As soon as they had parked, Gwen grabbed him again.

94

"You *did* have a good time, didn't you? You liked them, didn't you?"

"They're nice. Sure, I had a great time. It's a good bunch of kids."

"Whom did you like the best? First the guys. Which guy did you like the best?"

Jack was silent for a moment, then he said, laughing as he did, "I don't know. I liked them all. As I said, they're a good bunch."

Gwen kissed his cheek. "But there must have been one you enjoyed more than the others."

Jack thought again. "I guess so. I guess the guy we sat with while we ate."

"Joe Innes?" Gwen asked.

"Is that his name?"

Gwen was surprised. "Sure it's his name. You were calling him Joe all night."

"That's what's important, isn't it, to remember someone's name while you're with him. It makes him feel good. It makes him like you."

"Is that why you remembered everyone's name? To make them feel good and like you?"

Jack held her against him. "Anything wrong with that? It's what good politicians do all the time."

Gwen pushed a little away from Jack. "You asked Joe for his last name. You said you'd call him soon. Will you?"

Jack shrugged. "Probably not. It just seemed like a friendly thing to do."

Gwen looked out of the window at the navy-blue sky, filled with stars. "And Manda. Did you like her?"

Jack tightened. "Manda is OK. A little too smart for me. I don't mean that you aren't. You're probably smarter than she is, but she puts me off."

"Why?"

"I don't know. She just makes me uncomfortable. I don't

mean that we can't double if you want, just not often."

Gwen was about to answer when Jack kissed her. For a moment, her mind was with Manda, but then all she was aware of *was Jack's hand on her neck*, moving up into her hair. They kissed and held each other until he drove Gwen home.

At Gwen's house, Jack smiled at her, smoothed back his hair, and turned to her with that irresistible grin. "Tell you what. Next week it's your turn. My friend Harry Mitchell is giving a thing. We'll go to it, and you can see how I live."

As she got ready for bed that night, she thought of how their relationship was progressing. He had met her friends. He wanted her to meet his. They were moving closer and closer to each other.

In bed, Gwen couldn't sleep. She thought of how she felt when Jack kissed her . . . and yet . . . something seemed strange. Was it something in her? In Jack? She needed to talk to someone, just to stop her brain from sweeping in such widening circles. Someone older maybe. Her mother? She laughed out loud at the thought. Manda? Manda didn't know anything more than she did. Maybe Vivian. But Vivian was part of the whole mother syndrome to Gwen. Once a mother, always a mother, even if she was someone else's mother.

Adrienne? The idea so startled her that she sat up in bed. Gwen fell asleep shocked that she had thought, even for a second, that Adrienne could help her with anything, ever.

—— ♥ ——

The next day, Gwen walked over to Manda's, eager to talk about the party, to talk about Jack. Manda was stretched out on her lawn, trying to get an early start on a sun tan. She looked up as Gwen stood over her and smiled.

Gwen sank down on the green, soft beginnings of a lawn and sighed. "Did you really like him?"

"Sure. He's fine. But he doesn't think much of me. Right?"

Gwen was startled by Manda's astuteness. She had never lied to Manda and didn't want to now, even to protect Jack. "You make him uncomfortable, he says. He thinks you're too smart."

Manda sat up and ran her fingers through the grass. "I'm not smarter than you. Just smart in a different way."

"What do you mean *'different way'*?"

Manda shrugged. "I'm street smart. You're not."

Gwen laughed out loud. "*Street* smart? You've grown up in this town, middle class as can be, so how are you street smart?"

Manda thought for a while and then said, "I guess because I had a father who split. That makes you smart in a terrible way. I guess because I'm Jewish. Once a friend of my grandmother's came here with her. The lady had a number tattooed on her arm."

"Why would she have *that* done?"

Manda looked at Gwen. "She didn't *have* it done. She was in a concentration camp during World War II and the Nazis did it to her . . . to all the Jews. When I looked at that number, I thought, 'That could happen to me.' That makes you street smart too. In an awful way."

Gwen felt a wave of discomfort, of fear, begin at her toes and slowly move up her body. "You *don't* like him, do you?"

"Gwen, he's your guy. I don't have to like him; you do."

"But I want you to like him. Why don't you?" Gwen persisted.

Manda shifted on the grass and looked away . . . then back at Gwen. "I'm not sure. It isn't that I don't *like* him . . . he's likable. But he makes me uncomfortable, the way I make him. But that's OK. He's your boyfriend and I want you to be happy."

Gwen stared down at her hands. "I wanted my best friend

and my boyfriend to like each other."

Gwen stood up and walked away, her shoulders slumped. Manda stared after her and when Gwen turned around to look back, Manda blew her a kiss. Something she hadn't done since they were kids. Gwen smiled and waved weakly.

— ♥ —

Gwen was like a coiled spring when she and Jack drove to the party Saturday night. She had spent hours getting dressed, wanting to look better than she ever had for Jack's friends.

In the car going to Harry Mitchell's, Jack said, "I've never seen you so up tight. What's going on?"

"I want so much for your friends to like me."

"Of course, they'll like you. Why shouldn't they? Relax."

Harry Mitchell's house was small and there seemed to be kids in every corner, eating, talking, snuggling and in the middle of the living room two couples danced slowly, almost glued to each other.

Jack took Gwen around and introduced her to more people than she could remember. He kept his arm around her shoulders and said all the appropriate words, then he drifted off and Gwen watched him move from group to group. He smiled and they smiled. He talked and they slapped him on the back. The girls looked up at him, almost all with an overt or casual flirtatiousness. He didn't stay with one group very long, but moved constantly, leaving the kids looking after him with undisguised admiration as he walked away. Sometimes one or two followed him, trying to continue the conversation.

Gwen began to feel alone and left out when a girl came over to her and said, "He's something. Isn't he?"

Tessa Owens sat next to Gwen in math. Gwen was surprised to see her and glad, though she hardly said more than "Hi" to her in school.

"I didn't expect to see anyone I knew here," Gwen said.

"I date Harry Mitchell," Tessa said. "You're Jack O'Neal's girl, aren't you?"

Gwen had always hated that expression. Whenever anyone said about a girl, "Oh, she's so-and-so's girl," Gwen always wanted to say, "No! She is her *own* girl. No on can be someone else's girl."

But now Gwen had to admit to herself she liked the words "Jack O'Neal's girl." She hated herself for feeling that way, but she did.

"Yes, I see Jack a lot," Gwen answered.

Tessa watched Jack laughing, moving gracefully, pushing his hair off his forehead. "You're lucky. He's one of the cutest guys around."

Gwen was irritated by the look in Tessa's eyes . . . *pure yearning*. But she didn't know what to say. As she tried to put a few well-chosen words together, Jack came over and put his arm around her.

"Having a good time?"

"I'd have a better time if you'd stick around a little." Partly she was taking out her irritation with Tessa on Jack, and partly she was really annoyed with him. She hated being left to stand like a dummy among people she didn't know.

"I'm sorry," Jack said curtly. "Come on, we'll dance."

The evening was not a big success for Gwen. She felt left out and awkward and wished she were home. And she knew that Jack was aware of her feelings. When he drove her home, he said. "Look, Gwen, you're not a child. You don't have to have someone hold your hand at a party."

Gwen couldn't ever remember hearing that tone in his voice. "I know I'm not a child, but when I don't know people, I find it hard just to mingle. You do it well but I don't."

Jack smiled, "I saw you talking to Tessa whatever her name is. You mingled."

"Sure we talked. Mainly she told me how cute she

thought you were. Hardly what I want to hear from some girl who can't keep her eyes off you."

As Jack put his arm around Gwen, the identification bracelet on his wrist caught the glow from the passing street lights and shot slivers of brilliance into the car. "You're jealous, Gwennie . . . and I love it."

Gwen put her head on his shoulder and thought, *and I hate it*.

CHAPTER *13*

It was raining when Gwen left school on Monday. A misty drizzle fell softly on her, so gentle that she turned her face up to it, letting it almost caress her. Jack stood at his wall, just as the first time he had been there, with nothing on his head. Today his face and shirt were covered with the fine, sweet rain. He seemed always to be part of the weather, never resisting it.

They ran to his car, and he drove to a secluded spot in a wooded area. "No beach today," he said regretfully.

He pulled Gwen into his arms and she let her body sink into the warm dampness of his clothes. "I have to tell you, I'll be away a couple of days. My dad and I are going fishing."

Gwen pulled out of his arms. "Fishing? But you'll miss school."

"So I will," Jack said, smiling.

Gwen bit her lip. Why did she always have to say something to him that sounded so prissy, so goody-goody? It enraged her.

"Where are you going?"

"My folks have a small house up on Carter Lake. The weather is getting warm enough to fish all day, so Dad and I are just taking off. We're going tonight and we'll come back Wednesday night."

Gwen couldn't help thinking that only for a major crisis would her parents let her take off two school days. Fishing would never fall into the major-crisis area.

"I'll miss you," Gwen said wistfully.

"I'll miss you too. But I'll call you tomorrow night and when I get back Wednesday. And I'll bring you a fish."

Gwen wrinkled her nose. "I've never understood why people who wouldn't think of hunting feel it's OK to fish. I mean, is a hook in a fish's mouth less appalling than a bullet in a deer?"

Jack shrugged. "We're going to eat the fish. Some of them anyway."

"Yes, but that's not *why* you fish, is it? You fish for the pleasure of catching the poor thing on the hook and hauling it in. Probably the more it fights the more you enjoy it."

"The fish doesn't know what's happening to it. It probably doesn't feel a thing."

"How do you know?"

Jack laughed and rumpled Gwen's hair. "I'll ask the next live fish I see. How's that?"

Gwen burrowed into Jack's arms and laughed too. "I sound very silly to you. Don't I?"

Jack nodded. "You do, absolutely. I sometimes think you and I come from different planets."

"Then why do you want to be with me?" Gwen asked, dreading his answer . . . or really dreading his saying he didn't *know* why.

"I want to be with you, I guess, *because* you seem so alien to me. Because you think about so many things that I don't care about. It's not like any relationship I've ever had with a girl before."

Gwen giggled softly. "You mean I'm like an article in some sociological text book. 'Read about the strange creatures in Seaview.' "

But Jack didn't answer. He just kissed her.

When Gwen left school the next day, the place where Jack usually stood was glaringly empty. It seemed ugly without him, as if the wall had no reason for being except for Jack. She went to her violin lesson but couldn't concentrate. She tried to do her homework when she got home, but it seemed unimportant with the picture of the empty wall cemented in her mind. She wondered what time he would call—not until after dinner, probably. Her need to talk to him was incomprehensibly great.

At nine that night, Gwen thought *now*. They probably eat dinner late, after fishing all day, and now he'll call. She went over all the amusing things she'd saved all day to say to him. Things to make him laugh, to make him forget she was the girl who hated fishhooks.

She went over to the window and looked at the dark, cloudless sky. Michael pulled up in his family's car to the front of his house and got out to look at a tire. *I haven't seen him in weeks*, Gwen suddenly remembered. Not even hanging over the hedge. *Oh, Michael, I've been a louse to you. I should have at least stopped by to talk. But you didn't stop here either. But why should you? I'm the one who dumped you.*

She missed him acutely for a stabbing moment. She missed the ease, the sureness of their relationship, the feeling that they knew each other inside and out, that there were no surprises, the almost boring calmness she felt with him.

She got undressed and climbed into bed. Once again she watched the shadows of passing cars on the ceiling; once again she heard the stillness of the streets. At long last, she fell asleep, waking up suddenly, much later. It was 3:00 A.M. Even Jack O'Neal wouldn't call at that hour. She pushed up her pillows and sat up in bed, a feeling of numbness overpowering her. She couldn't even say she hurt; she felt like an observer, not part of the world at all. And what she was observing was a boy who seemed unbound by promises, by someone's expectations. At that moment, *he* was the alien, not she. Then the numbness left and fear took its place. *I'll never understand him. Never.*

After school the next day, without thinking or analyzing, Gwen got on a bus and went to Adrienne's. If anyone had asked why, Gwen would have had to answer that she had no idea why she wanted to be with Adrienne. Blood tie? Older, but not a mother figure to her? Accepting? Who knew? Who cared? Gwen followed her need.

Adrienne's eyes widened when she opened the door and saw Gwen. "Hi. What's up?"

Davey was playing on the floor of the living room and Gwen went over and kissed the top of his head. He reached up, grabbed a handful of her hair, and pulled, smiling broadly.

"I think he has a hair fetish," Adrienne said. "If we're lucky he'll be a world famous hairdresser; if we're not he'll just be a hair weirdo."

Adrienne hovered near the kitchen. "Coffee? Tea? Coke? Milk?"

Gwen shook her head. "I guess you wonder why I called this meeting," she said trying to joke, to figure out herself why she was there.

Adrienne sank down into a large chair. "Sort of. But, whatever, I'm glad you're here."

Gwen sat on the couch and stared at her hands. "It's Jack."

"I figured," Adrienne said.

And it all rushed out. All of Gwen's feelings, all of Jack's actions that puzzled and hurt her, up to the absence of a call the night before. And then, to complete Gwen's outpouring, she talked about her attraction to Jack, an attraction she had felt for no other boy.

Adrienne just listened and when Gwen was silent, she said softly, "Wow."

"That's all you have to say, 'wow'?" Gwen asked.

"Give me a second to get myself together. I'm not an advice-to-the-lovelorn expert or a trained psychologist or a palm reader."

Gwen got up angrily. "You're no help. I don't know why I thought you would be."

"Can it, Gwen. You know we're not exactly used to talking to each other. I'm feeling my way, sort of."

Gwen looked at Adrienne's wide eyes, filled with confusion and caring too. "I'm sorry, A. Really. Just say what you think."

"I think Jack is just irresponsible. He does his thing. The world is full of guys like that and it's usually girls like you who are attracted to them. It's not so terrible. So he forgets to call you once in a while. It would be a relief if Joe forgot something some times. You know it would add a little spice to life." She smiled.

"You wouldn't think so, if Joe were just your boyfriend and not your husband. You know Joe is coming home at night, no matter what."

"Maybe. But Jack seems like fun and he's good-looking and foxy."

Gwen's face was pale and drawn. "I don't know. He's also so removed from everything I think is important."

Adrienne walked over to Davey and put the pacifier he had lost back in his mouth. "The only bit of invaluable advice I can give you is, don't let yourself be pressured into doing anything you don't really want to. I've seen girls who have and they usually regret it."

"I guess. But Jack might just wander off, if I don't . . . you know . . . please him."

"Well, he'd wander off anyway then. Really."

Gwen stood up. "What do you know? You're only 20. And you've been married forever."

Adrienne laughed. "Being married doesn't necessarily make you dumb."

Gwen felt awkward. She wanted to leave but didn't know how suddenly just to take off politely. But Adrienne did it for her. "Go home. You want out of here. Right?"

"Yes. I don't know why. But it's as if my head is too full."

Jack didn't call that night either. Gwen didn't even know if she had expected him to or not, but she felt an anguish of disappointment.

But he *was* at the wall the next afternoon. He kissed her cheek, grabbed her hand, and walked her to his car. "Miss me?" he asked.

Although Gwen remained silent, he didn't seem to notice. He drove without asking to her spot on the beach, pulled out a bag from the back of the car, and walked to her dune. There he opened the bag and took out two Cokes.

Gwen took a long drink from hers and said as calmly as she could, "You didn't call Tuesday night or last night either. You said you would."

Jack thought for a few minutes. "Let's see. Oh, sure I called Tuesday night, but your line was busy. And last night . . . well, we just got home too late."

You're lying, Gwen thought, *no one called me Tuesday night at all, so the line couldn't have been busy.* Last night, OK, maybe it was too late. She was just about to argue with him about Tuesday, when he looked at her for a long moment, grabbed her hands, and held them tightly between his own.

"The lake is gorgeous, Gwen. You have to see it. Come up with me and my parents next weekend."

"You'll like them. They'll love you. Say yes." It spilled out of him in almost incoherent haste.

Gwen felt joy saturated with relief that made her almost speechless. He wanted her to meet his parents, wanted her to spend a weekend in his house. You couldn't ask a boy to prove what he felt for you in any more definite way than that. She threw her arms around his neck and hugged him as tightly as she could.

"I'll have to ask my mother, but I'm sure it will be OK. Oh, Jack, I'd love it, especially getting to know your parents. Jack, I'm happy, happy, happy."

She got up and whirled around the beach, finally sinking down into the sand, laughing. Jack flung himself down next to her and she hardly knew what made her happier, the smell of the sea in his hair and the loving look in his eyes, or knowing that he had asked her to come to the lake and meet his parents. All she knew was that she was experiencing a kind of joy she had never felt before and that Jack O'Neal was the reason for it.

— ♥ —

It didn't go quite as easily with her parents as Gwen thought it would. When she told them at dinner that night that Jack had invited her for a weekend, they exchanged a funny look.

"No," Gwen said. "It's not like that. His parents are going to be there too. We won't be alone, so relax."

"Where is this house?" Celia Warren asked.

"Somewhere on Carter Lake. I'm not sure exactly where."

Gwen's mother stirred her coffee thoughtfully. "I'd like to talk to Jack's mother first. Then we'll see."

Gwen stood up, outraged. "*Talk to Jack's mother*? You are practically medieval. You couldn't really *conceive* of embarrassing me that way."

"Gwen, calm down," her father said. "Your mother is perfectly right. We hardly know Jack and you don't even know where the house is. I think we should talk to one of his parents."

Gwen threw her napkin on the table and furiously started to clear away the dishes. "You treat me like a baby. I don't remember you carrying on like this when Adrienne was my age. *She* could do anything she wanted."

Mrs. Warren got up and grabbed a plate from the table. "*Adrienne* was not going off for weekends at boys' houses when she was your age."

"Of course not," Gwen shouted. "Adrienne was perfect.

107

She always was and always will be."

How did Adrienne get into this? Gwen wondered, knowing she had nothing to do with this situation. She was just a convenient thing to throw into the argument, perhaps as a way to try to make her mother feel some unthought-out guilt.

"What on earth has Adrienne to do with this?" Celia Warren asked, echoing Gwen's thoughts.

"*You know*," Gwen said with a deliberate and mysterious tone. Then she ran up to her room. What did she know? she thought. I'm really weird.

But it all worked out in some miraculous way. Gwen's mother talked to Mrs. O'Neal and was reassured that Gwen was welcome, would be looked after, and returned in one piece.

Jack drove Gwen up to the lake after school on Friday in his own car. His parents had gone early in the day and Gwen was glad for the time she was alone with Jack, time to get herself ready for the meeting with his parents.

"You know, you've never told me what your father sells . . . for a living I mean."

Jack kept his eyes on the road. "He's an insurance salesman, one of the best, too. If he wanted to, he could sell anything to anybody. He's hard to resist when he's 'on.' "

Gwen thought of her own father, funny and dear, but never "on." Usually buried under piles of papers filled with figures. "Not like my father, you mean."

Jack laughed. "They're different, all right. Both great, but different."

The O'Neal house, nestled in a grove of pine trees on the shore of Carter Lake, looked as if it had come out of a fairy tale—small and white with pink shutters. Gwen took a deep breath as she went in the door, crossing her fingers at the same time. *Let them like me*, she thought.

As soon as he saw her, Jack's father came over. He took her

hand and looked straight into her eyes. "Jack told me you were pretty, but he should have said beautiful."

Gwen flushed, but felt adult and desirable. "Thank you, Mr. O'Neal," she said and smiled over his shoulder at his wife.

"No. No. None of this Mr. O'Neal stuff. My name is Ira. You don't want to make me feel elderly, do you?"

Gwen smiled again and quickly took stock of Ira O'Neal. One of the handsomest men she had ever seen, he was put together in an entirely different way from Jack. He was very large and very tall, with bright-blue eyes and dark hair. A wiry mustache almost covered his upper lip, making his mouth, which was well-shaped and sensual, the first thing you noticed about his face. He filled the room with his largeness and vitality and deep voice; other people faded away when Ira O'Neal was there.

Still holding Gwen's hand, he took her over to Mrs. O'Neal. "Nancy, meet Gwen. Isn't she a beauty?"

Nancy O'Neal extended a small, white hand and as Gwen shook it, she became aware first of its softness and then of an underlying strength that surprised her. Mrs. O'Neal's petite frame seemed dwarfed by her husband's overwhelming stature and personality. From her, Jack had gotten the caramel-colored hair and golden eyes, but that was their only resemblance. She appeared to possess no grace and seemed to retire slightly at the same time she moved forward to Gwen.

"I'm glad you're here, Gwen. Let me show you to your room."

Gwen picked up her knapsack and followed Nancy O'Neal into a small room containing only a bed, a bureau, and one chair. Despite the sparseness of the furnishings, the warm colors of the bedspread, curtains, and hooked rug made it extremely cozy and comfortable.

"It's lovely," said Gwen softly.

"Good. The bathroom is right next door. If you need anything, just ask for it. Dinner will be in ten minutes."

Gwen unpacked the few things she had brought, washed her hands, and went into the living room where Mr. O'Neal was having coffee.

"Where is Mrs. O'Neal?" she asked. "I have just a little gift for her." Gwen had a small package in her hand. Her mother had bought it, insisting Gwen bring something with her.

"Her name is Nancy and she's in the kitchen fixing us a feast, I hope."

Gwen went in the direction Ira O'Neal pointed and found a large kitchen that looked like someone *was* preparing a feast. On one side, a round table was set with good china and fresh flowers. Gwen handed the package to Jack's mother. "This is for you, Mrs. O'Neal—just a little something."

"Jack's father would really like it if you would call us Ira and Nancy. Does that bother you?"

Gwen shrugged. "I'm not sure, but I'll try, if you really prefer it." *Oh, wow*, she thought.

Nancy opened the wrappings and took out a box of English soap, each bar wrapped in pastel paper and exuding a sweet floral odor that filled the area. "It's lovely, Gwen. Thank you. How did you guess I like unusual soaps?"

Gwen smiled. "My mother picked it out," she admitted. "*She* must have guessed." Gwen looked around the kitchen. "May I help with something?"

"No, you be a guest. Go sit with Jack and Ira. I have everything under control.

In ten minutes they were all seated at the table, which was almost sinking under a huge turkey, mashed potatoes, two vegetables, salad, and what looked like home-baked bread. Mr. O'Neal filled the delicate glasses and raised his. He looked at Gwen in a way that eliminated Jack and Nancy O'Neal from the room. "Welcome."

During dinner Ira O'Neal told them wonderful, funny stories about his attempts to sell various people insurance policies. Every now and then, he'd ask Jack a question about something or smile at Gwen. The house seemed to be too small to contain his charm and vibrancy. He should have been at a formal dinner somewhere, sitting next to men in tuxedoes and women with elegant dresses and diamonds wound in their hair. Gwen could hardly take her eyes from him and Jack hung on almost every word. Nancy O'Neal ate quietly, pushing the bowls of food toward her husband when his plate became empty. At one point she got up and brought a small plate of pickles to the table and placed it next to Ira. But she remained out of the flow of the conversation. Once she met Gwen's eyes and smiled warmly, but otherwise she watched her husband and ate.

When they had finished apple pie and coffee, Ira pushed his plate back from him and sighed. "All right, Jack. Why don't you and I go in the living room and let the ladies finish up?"

Jack raised his hand in Gwen's direction and followed his father out of the room. *Victorian*, Gwen thought, *the men going off somewhere, leaving the ladies to do their lady things*. But Ira O'Neal did it with such assurance that it was obvious he was used to and expected such behavior. Gwen sat at the table for a moment and then was aware of Nancy looking at her.

"It's done differently in your house?"

Gwen understood what she meant. "Well, yes. My father usually helps unless he has work that has to be done for the next day. But," she added hastily, "everbody doesn't do what we do. Kind of to each his own, I guess."

Nancy O'Neal smiled. "Ira always does his own thing, no matter what. Jack, too."

They did the dishes as quickly as they could. Nancy O'Neal asked Gwen questions about her life and seemed to be genuinely interested. But Gwen felt tense, eager to be intelligent and lively, and feeling she wasn't at all.

When they strolled into the living room, Jack and Ira were watching a baseball game on television. "Come sit down, Gwen, dear. Watch the game with us," Ira said.

Although Gwen didn't care much one way or the other about baseball, she dutifully watched the set and made appropriate comments. Jack and his father both seemed mesmerized, but made small talk with Gwen when nothing exciting was happening. Meanwhile, Nancy O'Neal read the newspaper in a corner chair, never looking at the TV screen.

At ten-thirty, Mr. O'Neal reached over and turned off the set. He stood up and smiled down at Jack. "Well, Jack, boy, we should turn in. If we're getting up at five to fish, we need a good night's sleep."

Gwen turned to Jack and raised her eyebrows, feeling both disbelief and fear. He couldn't be going off for the day and leaving her here.

Ira caught the look she was giving Jack and said warmly, "You and Nancy can spend the day shopping in Uniontown. They have a wonderful new mall there—really something to see." Then he reached into his pocket, took out his wallet, and handed Nancy what Gwen could see was a hundred-dollar bill. "Buy something for yourself that you really want, sweetheart."

Gwen had to fight hard to keep the tears from welling up in her eyes but she didn't say anything because she knew her voice would be shaky and filled with anger.

Jack reached for her and pulled her from her chair. "Come on, I'll take you down to the lake for a moonlight look. It's beautiful."

Ira O'Neal came over to her and gave her a hug. "Sleep well, little girl. We'll be back by six tomorrow and I am going to take the lot of us out for the best steak dinner around here. Nothing is too good for my women."

As soon as Gwen and Jack were a safe distance from the house, Gwen said, "You're not *really* going fishing for the whole day and leaving me with your mother?"

"Gwen, baby, that's what we come up here for . . . to fish. You know that."

"Yes, Jack, but *I'm* here with you this weekend. It's different. I want to *be* with you."

Jack pulled her close to him. "Baby, you *are* with me, right now. And you will be. We'll be back for dinner and we'll have all day Sunday together."

"But . . ." Gwen stopped, not knowing what else to say.

Jack asked quickly, "You like my mom, don't you? You'll enjoy being with her, won't you?"

Gwen felt caught in a net that she had no idea how to escape. What could she say? That she didn't feel relaxed with Jack's mother; that Nancy O'Neal was a stranger who couldn't be too eager to spend an entire day with Gwen either. Or that she hadn't come all this way to go to a shopping mall in Uniontown. "Of course, I like her, Jack. She's kind and nice, but . . ."

Jack kissed her nose. "Then everything is fine. We'll all have a great day."

The lake was shining under a half moon. The gentleness and calm of it touched Gwen, it was so different from her ocean—just a soft lapping of water against the tiny beach, no surge, no fighting to get to the shore and tugging to get away. The peacefulness of the water, the lack of turmoil in it reached Gwen. And when Jack pulled her into his arms, she just let herself sink against him. His hands wound into her hair and held her tightly. What did it matter? So he'd go fishing. He'd be back. It didn't matter, didn't matter.

As Gwen lay in bed that night, she knew Jack was in the room next to hers. She thought she could almost hear him breathing. She wondered if he were awake, too, if he were as aware of her as she was of him. She put her hand against the wall that separated her room from Jack's and willed some kind of waves to seep through the wall and encircle him. Then she sat up in bed and put her cheek against the wall; she could feel his arms around her and his hand on her shoulder. She tried not to think about the next day.

CHAPTER 14

When Gwen got up at eight-thirty, Jack and his father had gone and Nancy O'Neal was baking. Gwen showered, dressed, and walked into the kitchen. Nancy was bending over the oven and turned when she heard Gwen.

"Did you sleep well?"

Gwen nodded. "Fine." She felt awkward, not knowing what she was going to talk to this woman about all day. With the awkwardness came a surge of anger at Jack for putting her in this situation.

"Sit down. I'll make you breakfast," Mrs. O'Neal said. "What would you like?"

Gwen moved to the stove quickly. "Please, let me."

"OK. There are eggs and fresh orange juice in the refrigerator. The coffee is on the stove, the bread in the breadbox, but I really like making breakfast for guests."

Gwen poured coffee and put toast in the toaster. The juice was cold and sweet. Fresh orange juice was something her mother didn't bother with often.

"What would you like to do today, Gwen? We don't have to go to the mall, you know."

I'd like to go home, Gwen thought. *Or disappear. Or go back in my room and cry.*

"Anything, really," Gwen said. "Whatever you'd like." Decide, she silently begged Mrs. O'Neal. Don't let's stand around being polite.

Nancy sat down at the table with a cup of coffee. "Well, we

could just stay here and swim. Or we could go shopping. Or
. . . there's a wonderful little reconstructed town about 20
miles away. It's been rebuilt to be just like a colonial town—
houses, little stores, schoolhouse—more or less like Wil-
liamsburg. We could go there."

"I'd like that," Gwen said quickly. *Anything is better than
staying here alone with you*, she thought.

The day turned out to be almost fun for Gwen. Nancy
O'Neal was easy to be with and didn't expect a constant flow
of conversation, so the hours went by rapidly with a mini-
mum of discomfort. By the time they got back to the lake, at
four-thirty, Gwen felt at ease with Mrs. O'Neal.

"I'm going to have a swim before Jack gets back. If that's
OK with you," Gwen said.

"Fine. But be careful. There is more of a pull in the water
than you'd think."

Gwen smiled. "I'm an ocean girl. I'm used to tides and
pulls."

"You're in for a different kind of swimming then."

The lake was soft and sensual. The water seemed almost
to caress with its gentleness. It was clear and greenish, but
quite deep, so that though Gwen dove into it, she could see
no bottom, only dark, moving lines of water.

When she came back from the lake, she showered and
washed her hair, blowing it dry so that wild brown curls covered her head. She put on a yellow cotton dress and felt
ready for the best steakhouse in New York. When Gwen
wandered back out into the living room, Nancy was doing a
crossword puzzle.

Gwen flipped through a magazine lying on the couch and
at ten to six said, "They should be here any minute. They did
say six, didn't they?"

Nancy looked up. "Yes. Six is right."

Gwen went back to the magazine, trying to get interested
in an analysis of the Supreme Court structure—something

she knew she should read about if she were serious about becoming a lawyer. But the words remained separate words, never forming sentences or paragraphs. Finally, at six-thirty, she tossed the magazine down on the couch and walked to the window. The road that wound through the trees up to the O'Neal house was empty and silent.

"Do they fish far from here?" Gwen asked.

"Sometimes. They go wherever they think the fish will be biting best. Often that takes them quite a distance. Don't worry, Gwen, they'll be here. They probably ran into traffic."

At seven, Gwen felt the beginnings of the iciness that had become so familiar. Mrs. O'Neal had taken out the ironing board and was pressing some clothes. Gwen watched her as she meticulously moved the iron back and forth, totally at ease. It didn't seem to bother her that they had said six and it was now seven.

"Could they have had an accident?" Gwen asked. Her voice was shaky. "I mean if there's a lot of traffic, they could have been in an accident."

Nancy O'Neal shook her head, never looking up from the ironing board. "They didn't have an accident. Believe me."

At eight, Gwen flipped off the television set. She had been sitting for an hour watching people and words drift across the screen and not knowing anything she saw. She jumped up from her chair and stood in front of Mrs. O'Neal, who was still ironing.

"How can you be so calm? They are *two* hours late. *Two hours.* Doesn't it bother you at all?" Gwen didn't try to hide her anger and confusion.

"No, I'm not worried, if that's what you mean." She went to the refrigerator and took out the turkey from the night before. "Let me fix you a sandwich, you must be hungry."

"I don't *want* a sandwich. I'm *not* hungry. I just want Jack to come home and not be lying dead in some car wreck somewhere." Gwen was almost shouting. She had forgotten that Nancy O'Neal was Jack's mother, someone she wanted to like her. All she knew was that she was frightened and upset and this woman was in the same boat Gwen was. Except Nancy O'Neal was in another boat altogether. Gwen's was rocking and buffeted and about to break up; Nancy's was drifting calmly down a gentle river.

"He's not lying in a wreck anywhere, Gwen. They'll be here when they get here."

And then Gwen knew. She faced Nancy and her voice was low with anguish. "It's happened to you before. Hasn't it? I mean, they do this. That's why you're so calm, why you aren't worried. Because this is the way they act, Jack and Ira. It happens a lot, doesn't it?"

"It happens," Nancy said, meeting Gwen's eyes directly and not flinching at the look she saw.

"A lot?" Gwen asked.

"Often," Nancy replied.

Gwen sank down onto the couch and just stared at Nancy O'Neal. "I don't understand you. This is all right with you? You don't mind? It doesn't make you furious?"

Nancy laughed, a short, sharp sound. "No, it's not all right with me. Yes, I mind, and no, it doesn't make me furious anymore. I'm used to it."

"I'd *never* get used to it," Gwen said angrily. "Why should *you*?"

"Gwen, life is all one big compromise. Nothing is perfect. OK? I have Ira and all the excitement and fun and vitality he brings into my home; the price I pay is this kind of thing. He's . . ."

"Irresponsible," Gwen said, "like Jack. I'm sorry. I know I'm being rude but . . ."

"You're not rude, Gwen. Yes, I guess they're both irresponsible, but, oh, so charming."

Gwen thought of Adrienne and Joe. Adrienne would

gladly make a compromise like this . . . maybe. She walked to the window and looked out into the growing darkness that held no sign of headlights.

"Are you surprised, Gwen? Hasn't Jack ever done anything to disappoint you before? I remember a phone call a number of weeks ago. You sounded very upset."

Gwen felt tears begin to trickle slowly, slowly, down her cheeks. Mrs. O'Neal moved over and took Gwen in her arms. "Are you in love with Jack, Gwen?"

"Yes," Gwen mumbled into Nancy O'Neal's shoulder.

"Then be ready to make the compromise if you want him. He'll never change, you know. Never."

Gwen sat up and brushed at her face angrily. "How do you know? Maybe if you don't just accept this kind of junk, if you fight it . . ."

Nancy smiled. "You get very tired and also get nowhere. I love Ira. I love his vibrancy and I've made my choice . . . the choice is to compromise. I don't have a man who says he'll be here at six and is here, but when he comes in, *whenever* it is, he will fill this house with his presence. As Jack will."

Gwen turned away from Nancy, not wanting her to see the tears that continued flowing down her face. "I'm going to lie down for a while," she murmured.

In her room, she stretched out on the bed and tried to think, but her brain was numb or closed down for the night or just not functioning. She was aware of the sound of crickets and the almost imperceptible swishing of the lake. I wish I were a lake instead of an ocean, Gwen thought. No roars, no pulls, no surges, just swish, swish, swish.

She must have dozed off, because she awoke to the sound of a car pulling up in front of the house, the slamming of doors, and then loud voices. She got up and stood in the doorway of the living room silently. Ira and Jack bounded into the room and Ira grabbed Nancy. "Darling girl, forgive me. We stopped fishing in plenty of time to get here by six.

But at the dock we ran into these two guys and we started talking. Well, you know, they said have a cup of coffee, and I figured one cup wouldn't hurt while we exchanged tall fish stories. And then one coffee and one story led to another and suddenly it was eight-thirty. Then this boy," he gestured toward Jack, "well, he had to find . . ."

Jack was staring at Gwen. Her dress was rumpled, her face tear-stained, and her hair tumbled. He moved toward her and took her in his arms. "Gwennie. I'm sorry," he whispered.

Gwen remained stiff in his arms, not saying anything. Then Jack held something toward her. It was a wreath of tiny yellow tea roses. He put it on her head gently. "Remember, you asked if you should bring your yellow dress."

Ira O'Neal laughed loudly. "*That's* what made us so late. Jack insisted we drive around until he found the yellow roses. Then he had to weave them into that wreath. It took forever. We would have been here half an hour sooner, but looking at Gwen, it was worth it."

Ira took Gwen and led her to a mirror. She looked at the girl standing there with a delicate ring of flowers in her hair. They were beautiful and their perfume intoxicated her slightly. As she touched them, she saw that behind her, reflected in the mirror, Nancy O'Neal was looking at her with a tiny smile at her lips. Nancy raised her shoulders in an unmistakable gesture of surrender.

Then Nancy became businesslike. "It's too late to go out for dinner, so I'll fix something for us here. Did you catch anything after all this?"

"Catch anything?" Ira repeated. "Tomorrow we will have the best fish dinner you have ever had. Six big fish is what we have, my darling."

Jack took Gwen's hand. "While you're fixing dinner, Mom, Gwen and I will go out for a few minutes."

He led Gwen out of the house. "You look like a princess in

that wreath, Gwen, with the moonlight shining on you." He held her and murmured words that she had never heard from him before. "I'll always love you, always want you. You're my girl forever, Gwen. My girl, my rock. You're everything I want."

With a small cry, Gwen turned her head to him and kissed him fervently, blotting out everything, except that he was here and she had a wreath of yellow roses in her hair that he had remembered would match her dress. Everyone made compromises. How much was a ring of yellow roses worth?

— ♥ —

When Gwen woke up in the morning, the lake was covered by a light, drifting mist. The sun was burning through the haze, touching the dew-laden branches of the trees and bushes, turning them into gleaming crystals. The world was silent until Ira and Jack walked up the wide path from the lake to the house. They had been swimming and both had towels slung over their shoulders. Their hair was wet and water dripped from their legs. Ira said something and Jack threw back his head and laughed. Then Ira put his finger to his smiling lips, warning Jack not to wake up the sleeping household. Ira's large body moved solidly next to Jack's smaller one, but in spite of Ira's size, he didn't overpower Jack, whose grace and ease were wonderful to see.

Gwen watched them until she heard Nancy moving around in the kitchen. Then, putting on shorts and a T-shirt, she wandered out of her room.

Nancy smiled at Gwen as she beat up the batter for waffles. "You can set the table if you want."

They didn't talk about the night before nor did Nancy mention the wreath of roses. When Jack and Ira had dressed and come into the kitchen, Nancy began to cook breakfast— a feast of bacon and waffles and fresh orange juice and bagels and Danish pastries, all washed down with hot coffee.

Jack sat next to Gwen and gave her huge, loving smiles all through the meal. Ira told them some of the fish stories from the day before and Gwen couldn't remember when she had felt so sparkling, so happy at breakfast. When they had finished eating, Ira pushed back his chair. "Come on, Jack. We'll go to town for the newspapers while the girls are cleaning up."

Gwen noticed that Ira's words, his naturally assumed schedule of events, didn't seem as unfeeling, as bizarre, as it had the night before. As she and Nancy scraped dishes and put them in the dishwasher and washed pots and pans, Nancy said, "It doesn't change, as I said." Gwen nodded but didn't answer.

By the time they had finished in the kitchen, Jack and Ira had come back with their arms laden. They had newspapers, fresh fruit they had bought at a stand on the road, a bag of candy bars, and an armful of pine branches that filled the house with their spicy odor. Ira bowed and handed Nancy the fruit and pine boughs. "For you, my lady." He gave Gwen the candy bars. "For you, my princess."

The day passed in a warm glow of sitting outside and reading the papers, swimming in the cold lake and frying the fish for lunch and eating until they could hold no more. It was filled with laughter and joking and Jack was always beside her. He seemed totally relaxed in expressing his feelings for her in front of his parents. His arm was around her, his hand on hers, his lips putting a light kiss on her cheek.

"Our Jack finally has good taste, right, Nance? Gwen is more beautiful, smarter, nicer than that Winnie Effron." Ira smiled at Jack who laughed. But Nancy gave Gwen a quick look.

"Who is Winnie Effron?" Gwen asked, not sure she wanted to know.

"She was the girl before you, but she can't hold a candle to you, Gwennie," Ira answered, leaning back in his chair and blowing cigarette smoke into the air.

Nancy bit her lip and then said, too loudly, looking at Jack's wrist. "You really *do* like the bracelet I gave you, Jack. You never take it off, even to swim. I must admit I'm pleased."

"Best present I ever got, Mom," Jack said, twisting the bracelet around as he spoke.

Gwen knew Nancy had tried to change the subject as diplomatically as possible, but the name echoed in her head— Winnie.

They left the lake at five. Gwen hated to go, feeling that Jack had never, except for leaving on his fishing expedition, been as loving, as close to her as he had that weekend.

As Gwen and Jack got into his car, Ira called out, "We'll meet at that hamburger place on Route #4. We can stop and have a little dinner before we get home."

Gwen put her head on Jack's shoulder as he drove, and sighed. "It was lovely. Really lovely."

Jack bent his head and kissed her cheek. "Good. My parents are great, aren't they?"

"Yes," Gwen answered. Then slowly, "Who is Winnie Effron?"

"She's nothing. No one. Just a girl I dated a little."

"Did you take her up to the lake too?" Gwen asked softly.

"Just once. It didn't work at all. She wasn't like you, Gwen. She was a real dud."

Gwen didn't ask how.

They drove in silence, enjoying the warm, sweet-smelling air and the gathering twilight. Then Gwen said, "I'm going to Adrienne's after school tomorrow. I want to pick up a paper she wrote on Emily Dickinson when she was in college. I'm doing one for my English class and maybe Adrienne had some ideas that would help me. Want to drive me over there?"

Jack thought for a moment. "Sure. I can do that."

Gwen felt a wave of relief. "We don't have to stay. We can just get the paper and leave."

"Listen," Jack said, "I'm stopping at Harry Mitchell's when we get back tonight. He was going to rent a video cassette of an old Bogart movie I wanted to see. Come with me."

"I can't, Jack. My mother expects me home and I have work to do for tomorrow."

Jack grinned. "Have to crack the old law books, eh?"

Gwen felt uncomfortable. "No, you know that isn't so, but I do have work to do." Why did he always make her feel so stodgy?

Jack squeezed her hand. "Tessa will be there. So you'll know someone besides me."

"I hardly know Tessa anyway. She just sits in front of me in French class. I can't, Jack. I can't go. Don't be angry."

"Gwen, I'm not angry. I just thought it would be a nice way to end the weekend."

At that moment they pulled into the hamburger place that Ira had mentioned. The meal was more laughter, more banter, and Ira seemed to devote himself to charming the waitress, who openly flirted with him. Gwen watched Nancy to see how she was reacting to this, but she just ate her food and looked around the restaurant, never letting her eyes fall on Ira or the waitress.

When Jack dropped Gwen off at her house, he took her in his arms and held her for a long moment. "It was wonderful being with you this weekend. You're great."

Gwen kissed him softly. "You're great too. More than great." She slipped out of the car and watched him drive away until the last glow of his taillights were gone.

As she turned to walk to her house, Michael came running down to the road. Going to meet a girl? Gwen wondered. He stopped when he saw Gwen. "I haven't seen you in a long time."

"I know," Gwen nodded. "I've looked for you, thought we could hang over the hedge and talk, but you're never around."

Michael gestured toward Gwen's knapsack. "Been away?"

Gwen felt suddenly ill-at-ease. "I was at Jack's folks' house up at Carter Lake. Just for the weekend."

She could see Michael clearly in the streetlight. He raised his eyebrows. "Getting serious, huh? When a guy asks a girl to meet his folks, well it says something."

Gwen laughed and shrugged. "I don't know. Maybe."

They looked at each other for a moment, and then Michael said, "I have to run. I'm meeting someone at the movies. See you Gwen."

"Yeah. Sure," Gwen said and turned to her house, thinking, was Jack serious with Winnie What's-her-name too?

CHAPTER 15

Manda was waiting for Gwen at the bus stop the next morning. "I walked three blocks out of my way just to make sure I saw you. So how did it go? What are they like? Did you have a good time?"

"In the order asked: It went fine, they were great, and yes."

Manda looked at Gwen with disgust. "More details, please. I have not come traipsing to your bus stop to hear puny little comments like that."

They got on the bus and sat down together, while Manda, as usual, started combing her hair, tucking her blouse in her jeans, and putting on eye make-up. "Give me a blow-by-blow from the first moment to the last."

Gwen started building up how charming Ira was, how nice Nancy was, how adorable the house was, and how loving Jack was. When she got to Saturday, she said quickly, "And I spent a wonderful day with Nancy. We went to this great little . . ."

Manda held up her hand. "Wait. Back up. Where was Jack?"

"Well, he and Ira had planned to go fishing, so . . ."

"He left you with his *mother* so he could *fish*?" Manda snorted. "Gwen, it's Manda. Come on now."

Gwen stared out the bus window. "OK. So I didn't like it, but what could I do? Anyway, yesterday was wonderful. We were together every second. He even kissed me in front of his parents. He made me this beautiful wreath of roses Saturday too. I still have it."

Manda was silent.

Gwen turned to her and said slowly, carefully. "It's the way he is, Manda. That's who Jack is. I take it or I leave it, as it is."

"You take a lot," Manda said.

"I get a lot too," Gwen answered quickly.

"If you call wreaths of roses a lot . . . it's your life," Manda said, "but . . ."

"You're right, Manda," Gwen said firmly. "It's my life."

— ♥ —

When Gwen came out of school that afternoon, Jack wasn't there. She leaned against the wall and waited, thinking, *If you didn't want to go to Adrienne's, why didn't you just say so.?* She looked in the direction from which Jack would arrive, willing him to come striding toward her. A weekend with his parents and he flaked out again. Who was he? What did he feel?

Gwen waited 15 minutes and then ran to get the bus to Adrienne's. She looked back every few steps, yearning to see him, to hear him calling her name. She huddled in the lumpy seat, cold in spite of the warm May sun. Anger fought with pain, and despondency with hope. You compromise, Nancy O'Neal had said.

As soon as Adrienne opened the door, Gwen knew she shouldn't have come. She was filled with all the old jealousies and angers. Adrienne had what she wanted, why couldn't Gwen? Adrienne had the man she wanted, coming home every night. She wasn't waiting for phone calls, waiting for his appearance, playing second fiddle to a fish. All Gwen wanted to do was get the Dickinson paper and flee. Adrienne smiled and nodded her head in the direction of the living room.

It was quiet. "Where's Davey?" Gwen asked.

"Joe's mother took him for the day, just to give me time to

catch up on the laundry and other fascinating things like that."

Gwen sank down on the couch and looked at the usual mess in the room. Why can't she ever clean up? She's got a man who is always here, who loves her. Why can't she be neat? I would be if I were married to Jack.

"Want a Coke?" Adrienne asked. "Peanut-butter sandwich? Cookies?"

"Why?" Gwen exploded. "Why do you feel you have to stuff my mouth as soon as I walk in the door?"

Adrienne put her hands on her hips. "Why?" she yelled back. "Because I know you want *something* from me and I don't know what. I thought we were beginning to be friends, but you come in today looking as hateful as ever. What do you want from me?"

"You don't know anything," Gwen shouted. "You don't know what it's like to be in love and never know whether the guy is going to be there or not. You have it all. I want us to be close, but I don't know how when I always feel you're in a better place than I am. I want to *want* to tell you about Jack, and I don't want to tell you at all. I want a storybook sister."

"If you want a storybook sister, why do you always act like Cinderella and treat me like the wicked stepsister?"

Adrienne sat down next to Gwen and touched her arm lightly. "Look, we both want the same thing, so aren't we ahead? Isn't that a place to start? Can't we try again?" She hesitated. "What about Jack."

Too much is going on today, Gwen thought. "I'm sorry. I am. It's my fault, not yours. I know it. I want to try with you. I *need* to. But not about Jack today. I can't."

"OK," Adrienne said and smiled. "Want a peanut-butter sandwich?"

"No! No! I don't *want* a sandwich." Gwen was silent. Then, "Do you have any cheese?"

They laughed and Gwen got up. "Look, give me the Dickinson paper and let me go while we're ahead. Otherwise, I'll louse things up between us again. Let me go while we're still friends."

Adrienne found the paper and when she gave it to Gwen she asked, "Will you come back?"

"Yes," Gwen said. "I will. Really." And she meant it. At the door, she leaned over impulsively and kissed Adrienne's cheek. "Why isn't anything easy?"

Adrienne shrugged. "That's life, kid."

— ♥ —

Jack didn't call that night and to Gwen it seemed as if her arm were too heavy to reach for the phone to call him. She lay in bed awake until after two, imagining the ring that never came, and then finally fell asleep.

By the time Gwen walked into her math class the next day, she could hardly stay awake. She slipped into her seat and was aware of Tessa sitting in front of her, her perfume drifting back, making Gwen's head feel stuffed. The room was too warm, feeling more like the end of June than the end of May. Tessa wiggled in her seat and didn't seem to be able to find a comfortable position. She stretched her left arm along the back of her chair and Gwen admired a shiny bracelet on Tessa's wrist. She was almost hypnotized by the flashes of light the sun brought from the silver.

Then Gwen's eyes focused. The blood pounded in her ears—J. O'N. Those were the initials on the bracelet Tessa was wearing. Jack's bracelet. The one he never took off. Gwen looked away and then back at the bracelet. It was true . . . J. O'N. Suddenly, Gwen knew that Tessa had deliberately moved her arm into that position, wanted Gwen to see Jack's bracelet and to let her know that it was now Tessa's.

Just as time had stood still and had been forever for Gwen that first day in Dawson's, so it was now. She heard birds chirping outside; her math teacher's monotone voice; someone coughing in the hall. She saw the sun blazing into the room and the boy to her right making *drawings in his notebook*. And always the bracelet. *Jack,* she cried silently, *Jack. What are you doing?*

After class she went into the ladies' room and splashed cold water on her face. Then she went into a booth, put the lid down, and just sat on the seat staring straight ahead. She couldn't go to her last class. She couldn't. She sat in the booth for 45 minutes, listening to girls coming and going, laughing, joking, and then a girl weeping softly in the booth next to hers. When the bell rang, she got up and walked out of school.

Jack was there. The sun bathed him, making him more golden than ever. He kissed her cheek when she was next to him. "Sorry about yesterday. I got tied up."

Gwen didn't answer. Yesterday didn't matter. "Jack, Tessa has your bracelet on her wrist. How come?"

Jack laughed and put his arm around Gwen. "You know, it was one of those things. We were kidding around at Harry's Sunday night. She kept begging to try it on, so I gave it to her. Then she kept saying she couldn't get it off, running away when I tried to grab her arm. That kind of thing. So I figured what's the difference? It's only a bracelet."

"Your mother gave it to you, Jack." What a dumb thing to say, Gwen screamed to herself. Your world is falling apart and you say a stupid thing like, "Your mother gave it to you."

"She won't care," Jack said.

"I care," Gwen shouted. "Didn't you know Tessa would make sure I saw that bracelet?"

Jack looked surprised. "I didn't think about it. OK, so you saw it. Let her have the dumb bracelet. It doesn't mean anything."

"It does," Gwen continued yelling. "It means something to *me*.

Jack took a step back. "Look, Gwen, darling girl. I can't

stay this afternoon. I'm driving over to Mineola to get a tape deck for the car."

"Don't go yet, Jack. We have to talk."

Jack brushed a curl off Gwen's forehead. "I'll call you tonight. Eight on the dot. We'll talk forever." He kissed Gwen and walked away in that loose, easy way. She just stared after him, watching him.

When Gwen got home, she went up to her room and sat by the window. Michael was running in place on his lawn. Her mother was downstairs vacuuming the dining room. A kid went skateboarding down the street. Everything was the same. The world was still turning. What did it matter if Tessa had a bracelet that said J. O'N.?

While Gwen ate dinner with her parents, she never uttered a word. Celia and Ethan Warren exchanged looks and talked over her head, leaving her alone with her tumultuous confusion and feelings.

At seven she went back to her room and lay on the bed. It was warm but she pulled a blanket over her and huddled underneath it, waiting.

At eight o'clock on the dot, the phone rang. Gwen didn't look at it but she counted the rings. One, 2, 3, 4, 5, 6, 7, 8, 9, 10, 11. Each ring pierced her head or her heart, she didn't know which.

She clenched her hands together so that she wouldn't reach for the telephone. She bit her lower lip hard so that she could concentrate on some physical feeling. The phone was silent.

Suddenly her father appeared at the door to her room. "Your phone has been ringing like crazy. Didn't you hear it, Gwen?"

"I heard it."

Ethan Warren looked at his daughter. "So why didn't you answer it?" he yelled.

Gwen sat up and rocked back and forth on the edge of the

bed, her arms wrapped around herself. "Because!" she shouted. "Because I'm only 16 years old and I don't have to compromise yet. Do I? I *will* when I *have* to, but I don't have to yet. Do I?" She pleaded with her eyes and voice.

Her father looked down at her and said gently, lovingly, "I'm not sure what you're talking about. But no. You don't have to compromise yet, Gwen. Not yet."

He hovered over her, looking as if he were going to stay. Then he turned away and softly closed the door, giving Gwen the gift of privacy that she wanted at that moment.

CHAPTER 16

Jack was there the next afternoon, leaning against the wall, looking more appealing than Gwen could remember.

As soon as she reached his side, Jack said, "I called last night right at eight. Just like I said I would. But you weren't there."

"Yes, I was," Gwen said, her voice wavering.

"But you didn't answer," Jack said.

"I know," Gwen replied, staring over his head.

"Why?"

Gwen looked around her at the mobs of kids leaving school, pushing and laughing. *Is this how it's going to end? Is this how you break up with a boy you love, with a hundred other people all around you? But then is there a good way to break up with a boy you love?*

"Jack, please listen. We're too different. Or we don't really *go* together. Or something. I want things you don't even understand, so how can you give them to me?"

Jack looked at Gwen with disbelief. His golden eyes widened and then narrowed. "But I love you, Gwen."

"I know, Jack. I know. That's what makes it even worse. And I love you. But I can't be the way you need a girl to be in order to *be* your girl." Gwen felt her breath stick in her throat. "I hurt too much when I'm with you, Jack. And I don't want to." There was a desperation in her voice to which Jack responded.

He grabbed Gwen's hand and held it tightly. "Is it because of the bracelet? I'll get it back. *You* can have it."

Gwen shook her head. "It isn't the bracelet. Or it isn't *just* the bracelet. It's . . . it's . . . I can't explain so you'll understand, Jack. You won't know what I mean." Gwen was yelling now, appalled at the sound of her own voice.

"Come into the car so we can talk, Gwen."

"No," Gwen shouted. She knew if she got into the car, if she let him take her in his arms, she would be lost. "Jack, I can't see you any more. I'll die if I do, or something. I won't be myself. I won't even *know* me."

Jack looked over her shoulder, smiled at a boy walking by who had waved to him, and then he looked back at Gwen. He visibly straightened his shoulders and he grinned at her. "Whatever you want, Gwennie," he said in a firm voice, but his eyes were still disbelieving. "I'll call you, though."

"Please don't, Jack. Please don't," she begged.

He shrugged. "OK. If you change your mind, you call me then." He wanted to get away. It was apparent to Gwen that he'd never make too much effort to keep her.

"Sure," Gwen said.

"I'll be up at the lake with my dad for a few weeks once school closes. You know the old fishing bit."

"Yes, I know," Gwen said in a whisper.

Jack backed away from her a few steps, raised his arm, waved his hand in a breezy, stylish way, and walked away. Gwen watched him as she had so many times before. Watched the way he moved and the way he held his head, and she said in a soft voice, "Bye, Jack. Oh, Jack, good-bye."

She left the school grounds and started walking home, needing to move and not be cramped in the bus. She walked and then began to run as fast as she could. Faster and faster, trying to blot out everything but her moving legs.

"Want a lift?" A car slowed down near her.

Manda stopped her car as Gwen stopped running. Gwen hesitated and then said, "If you give me a hard time, I'll get right out."

"I haven't said a word," Manda yelled.

"But you will. You always do."

Gwen got in the car and huddled down in the seat, not talking. Then she said, "I broke up with Jack."

"I'm sorry," Manda said softly.

"Why? You didn't even like him."

Manda started the car. "But *you* did."

"No," Gwen said loudly. "I didn't *like* him. You're using all the wrong words. I *love* him. Right now, I love him."

Then she stopped talking and began to cry, loud sobs and keening wails that racked her body and shook the front seat of the car. She didn't try to wipe her nose or face and the tears raced down her cheeks. She gulped and coughed and groaned. Manda kept driving, never taking her eyes from the road, never saying a word. Gwen moaned slightly and then it all stopped. And she sat silently in the car.

"OK?" Manda asked.

"For now." Gwen watched the streets go by. "I'll never forget him. *Never*. If only he could have been just a little different. Just a little."

Gwen never saw him again. He never called. He never came to her school. Once she thought she caught a glimpse of him at a shopping mall, but the shining head she was watching disappeared in the crowd before she could be sure it was Jack O'Neal.

Later, much later, she would ask herself, "*Would I have gone to the beach that day had I known what was going to happen?*" The same answer always sang wildly in her head, "*Yes, oh, yes!*"

*ANN REIT has written several
successful romances for young adults.
She lives in New York City, where
she is an editor for a major
publishing company.*